NASHVILLE | BOOK EIGHT | R U SERIOUS

NASHVILLE | BOOK EIGHT | R U SERIOUS

INGLATH COOPER

Contents

Copyright

Books by Inglath Cooper

Swerve

The Heart That Breaks

My Italian Lover

Fences – Book Three – Smith Mountain Lake Series

Dragonfly Summer – Book Two – Smith Mountain Lake Series

Blue Wide Sky – Book One – Smith Mountain Lake Series

That Month in Tuscany

And Then You Loved Me

Down a Country Road

Good Guys Love Dogs

Truths and Roses

Nashville – Part Ten – Not Without You

Nashville – Book Nine – You, Me and a Palm Tree

Nashville – Book Eight – R U Serious

Nashville – Book Seven – Commit

Nashville – Book Six – Sweet Tea and Me

Nashville – Book Five – Amazed

Nashville – Book Four – Pleasure in the Rain

Nashville – Book Three – What We Feel

Nashville – Book Two – Hammer and a Song

Nashville – Book One – Ready to Reach

On Angel's Wings

A Gift of Grace

RITA® Award Winner John Riley's Girl

A Woman With Secrets

Unfinished Business

A Woman Like Annie

The Lost Daughter of Pigeon Hollow

A Year and a Day

Reviews

Readers who have enjoyed the emotional stories of authors like Colleen Hoover may enjoy this live-your-dream story where "Inglath Cooper draws you in with her words and her amazing characters. It is a joy to pick up these books. There is just the right amount of love and romance with the perfect dose of reality. The dialogue is relatable and you just fall in love with the story."

♪

"Truths and Roses . . . so sweet and adorable, I didn't want to stop reading it. I could have put it down and picked it up again in the morning, but I didn't want to." – **Kirkusreviews.com**

On Truths and Roses: "I adored this book...what romance should be, entwined with real feelings, real life and roses blooming. Hats off to the author, best book I have read in a while." – **Rachel Dove, FrustratedYukkyMommyBlog**

"I am a sucker for sweet love stories! This is definitely one of those! It was a very easy, well written, book. It was easy to follow, detailed, and didn't leave me hanging without answers." – **www.layfieldbaby.blogspot.com**

"I don't give it often, but I am giving it here – the sacred 10. Why? Inglath Cooper's A GIFT OF GRACE mesmerized me; I consumed it in one sitting. When I turned the last page, it was three in the morning." – **MaryGrace Meloche, Contemporary Romance Writers**

5 Blue Ribbon Rating! ". . .More a work of art than a story. . .Tragedies affect entire families as well as close loved ones, and this story portrays that beautifully as well as giving the reader hope that somewhere out there is A GIFT OF GRACE for all of us." — **Chrissy Dionne, Romance Junkies 5 Stars**

"A warm contemporary family drama, starring likable people coping with tragedy and triumph." 4 1/2 Stars. — **Harriet Klausner**

"A GIFT OF GRACE is a beautiful, intense, and superbly written novel about grief and letting go, second chances and coming alive again after devastating adversity. Warning!! A GIFT OF GRACE is a three-hanky read...better make that a BIG box of tissues read! Wowsers, I haven't cried so much while reading a book in a long long time...Ms. Cooper's skill makes A GIFT OF GRACE totally believable, totally absorbing...and makes Laney Tucker vibrantly alive. This book will get into your heart and it will NOT let go. A GIFT OF GRACE is simply stunning in every way—brava, Ms. Cooper! Highly, highly recommended!" – **4 1/2 Hearts — Romance Readers Connection**

"...A WOMAN WITH SECRETS...a powerful love story laced with treachery, deceit and old wounds that will not heal...enchanting tale...weaved with passion, humor, broken hearts and a commanding love that will have your heart soaring and cheering for a happily-ever-after love. Kate is strong-willed, passionate and suffers a bruised heart. Cole is sexy, stubborn and also suffers a bruised heart...gripping plot. I look forward to reading more of Ms. Cooper's work!" – **www.freshfiction.com**

★

CeCe and Holden have what is sometimes unusual in the entertainment world: a good marriage. They know how lucky they are to have found each other, and with the recent scare they witnessed best friends Thomas and Lila go through, they're determined not to take any of it for granted. But life in the public eye can come with its drawbacks, and when Holden begins to receive attention from a woman intent on having him, he's no longer sure the spotlight is worth it. CeCe refuses to let another woman's fixation determine how they live. But desire is a powerful force, and when a woman is willing to go to whatever lengths are necessary to get what she wants, the game suddenly has no rules.

And without rules, no one is safe.

♪

CeCe

LIFE IS A ROLLER COASTER.

The highs are so high. And the lows can be so low.

I'm not complaining. It's just a fact I've come to accept. And the past six months have definitely proven my theory true.

I look out the airplane window now at the puffy white clouds below and feel a stab of gratitude for how far Lila has come in the past six months. The setbacks have been terrifying, times when we were all so afraid that her body would reject her new heart. Only in the last month or two, have we all felt as if we could stop holding our breath and believe in the miracle Lila has been given.

I love her like a sister, and I can't even imagine what would have happened to Thomas if she had died. The truth is I think he would have died too of grief. You only have to look in his eyes to see that he knows second chances like this don't come along very often.

Our career in country music has been a roller coaster during this time as well.

Watching it continue to grow even though we're no longer with our original label has been immensely rewarding, especially for Holden. He's been the catalyst, determined to make it work, acting as our manager while writing at a pace he's never written at before. His determination has carried us during the time when Thomas has been unable and unwilling to focus on music.

My phone pings in my lap. I glance down at the screen. There's an iMessage text from Holden.

Hey, babe. How was the shoot?
It went well. Everyone at the magazine was really nice.
Glad to be out of NYC?
You know me. Country girl.
I'm missing my country girl.
Miss you too.
Your mom's picking you up at the airport, right?
Yes. Still no chance you can come for the weekend?

1

I can cancel the dinner and come to Virginia.

No. I want you to keep it. We need to bring in a manager so you can stop working as much.

The flight attendant announces over the intercom, "We'll be landing shortly. Please put away all electronic devices at this time."

Gotta go. Call you later.

Love you, babe.

Love you too.

♪

MAMA IS WAITING for me at the gate. We walk straight to each other, arms open. I step into her hug, closing my eyes and breathing in the familiar scent of her.

She leans back and pushes my hair away from my face in the same gesture she's used since I was a little girl. It always makes me feel loved, cherished.

"Hi, honey," she says. "I can't believe it's been three months."

"I'm sorry," I say, hugging her hard. "It's been kind of crazy."

"I understand," she says. "That wasn't chastising."

We walk to baggage claim, catching up on the recent trip she and Aunt Vera took to Las Vegas.

"Slot machines and free mai-tais?" Mama says, shaking her head and making a clucking noise. "You know that's not a good idea for our Vera."

I laugh. "I have to admit I was a little surprised you agreed to go."

"Imagine what would have happened if I hadn't been there."

"Aunt Vera does know how to keep the party interesting," I say.

My bag is on the carousel, and I lift it off, pulling it behind me to the parking spot in the airport garage.

During the thirty-minute ride home, she asks me dozens of questions, and I catch her up on what's been going on in our lives in Nashville. We talk for a good bit about Thomas and Lila. And she, like everyone who hears the story, responds with the same emotion for the dual nature of the outcome. Happiness for Lila's miracle and sadness for the tragedy that was her father's life.

I haven't actually been back home for a couple of years. As Mama turns the car into the driveway, I feel nostalgia for this place that holds so many memories for me.

I stare through the windshield at the modest brick house I had grown up in. "I'm sorry it's been so long since I've been here, Mama," I say. "I don't know how time passes so fast."

"It's all right," she says. "You know how much I enjoy my visits to see you and Holden in Nashville."

"You haven't been for a while though."

"Same thing here, you know. Life just gets so busy. Come on, let's get you inside and settled. I'm fixing you a big dinner. A good wind would blow you away, child."

I smile and get my bag from the trunk. "Hardly, Mama."

She opens the side door to the house, and we step into the kitchen. I breathe in the familiar scent of Mama's cooking. "Did you make a pie?" I ask, smiling.

"Two, actually. I couldn't decide if you would prefer the apple or the coconut cream."

"I'm glad you didn't make me choose," I say, smiling.

"I'm just going to finish up dinner. Your room is all ready for you."

"Thank you, Mama," I say, giving her a hug. "It's really good to be here."

"You just don't know how good it is to have you, honey."

♪

Holden

OUR HOUSE IS incredibly lonely without CeCe.

Hank Junior and Patsy follow me around from room to room in silent demand that I immediately tell them where she is.

"She'll be back soon, guys," I say, sitting down at my desk and tapping the space bar to bring up the computer.

Hank Junior makes a sound of discontent and drops on the floor next to my chair. Patsy curls up beside him as if she knows she's the only one other than CeCe who can comfort him.

I reach down and rub each of them, then turn my focus to the computer screen. I haven't checked our social media pages in a few days. I try to duck in on a daily basis. I figure if someone likes our music enough to publicly comment on it, we have a responsibility to respond to them.

I go through the Twitter feed, replying to comments and thanking people for their postings and retweets.

Facebook indicates 344 new notifications. I resolve to do a better job of getting in here everyday. I scroll through, looking for comments and replying to each one. Most are just polite and kind and make me newly grateful that we are able to do what we do for a living.

Creating music that people enjoy is something I don't ever want to take for granted. Fans have a lot to choose from these days. And easy access to entertainment of all varieties. It's not a given that they will continue to choose us as part of that.

So I thank them individually, reminding myself that it's this connection with music lovers that allows me to continue doing what I love.

I'm nearly at the end of the notifications list when I click on a comment for the post from a few days ago about CeCe's photo shoot in New York City. She's actually hamming it up with one of the helpers on the set. They're both making a silly face at the camera. The caption reads:

Missing my hubby and my dogs. But folks here are keeping me busy. And New Yorkers are really nice!

The post has more than 200 comments. I start to type in thanks to everyone who commented when one response catches my eye. I've seen the poster's name before and can't remember why something she said at some point bothered me. I click on the comment.

CeCe might be pretty enough for the photo shoot. But she's not pretty enough for you, Holden! If she's out of town, can I come over? ?

The replies to her comment vary from **Me, too!** to **Holden would never cheat on CeCe, skank!**

I decide I'm better off ignoring this one, but once I'm done looking through the other notifications, I go back to the poster's name and click through to her Facebook profile.

Charlotte Gearly. Age 23. Works at Ramsey Auto Parts. Franklin, Tennessee.

She's pretty. Dark hair. Wide white smile. Her self-confidence is evident in the first few photos visible in the feed. In the third one down, she's wearing a Barefoot Outlook T-shirt that fits her curves with the clear intent of displaying them. The caption on the photo says:

Holden Ashford. Sigh. One day. Mine.

I back out of the page, deciding not to give the statement any thought. Similar comments have been made by others about all three of us, and it seems like ignoring them is the best response.

I finish up with Facebook, check the band's email account, answer what's there and then push away from the desk.

Hank Junior and Patsy remind me it's time for their walk. I get their leashes from the bowl at the front door, and we head outside. The winter air is cold against my skin, and I say, "All right, you two, let's make this quick."

We walk down the driveway, both of them sniffing everything within reach of their nose. It's a hound thing, and not a routine either of them is willing to forgo once they're out the front door.

My phone dings and I look at the screen. It's CeCe.

Mama made me two kinds of pie.

I shake my head, texting back.

I knew I should have come.
Told you.
Which one was best?
Can't pick a favorite.
You're my favorite dessert.
From anyone else, I'd find that corny.
I wouldn't say it to anyone else.
That's why it's not corny. ?
What are you doing?
Walking my employers.
Giggle. We both work for them, don't we?
Hank is very outdone with you.
Tell him I'll be home soon.
I did. He's still not happy.
Poor Hanky.
We'll finish our walk and I'll call you in a bit.
K.

At the end of the driveway, we take a right onto the sidewalk. A car is parked alongside the street. The door opens, and someone gets out. Hank Junior barks his big hound bark.

"Come on, boy," I say, not really looking at the person.

"Hey, Holden." It's a woman's voice.

I stop and turn around, unable to make out the face in the dim light. "Ah, hey," I say, trying to figure out if I know her. She's wearing a baseball cap and a hoodie, and I wonder for a moment if I'm about to be robbed or something.

I start to walk on then, tugging Hank behind me. He's still making a low growling sound, something I've almost never heard him do.

"I came to see you," she calls out.

I stop now and turn back. "Quiet, Hank," I say. He looks up at me, as if questioning whether I really want him to stop or not. I rub his head and say to the woman, "Is there something I can do for you?"

She smiles and says, "Actually, I was hoping I could do something for you."

"I don't believe we know each other," I say.

"I know you. I own every song you've ever recorded and have been to every concert I could possibly make it to."

"Ah, thank you," I say. "But—"

"I know she's not here. CeCe, I mean."

"Look, I have to go—"

She walks closer, stopping a few yards away, as if she's not sure she should trust Hank's silence.

"Maybe I could come in for a bit and keep you company. Chase away the loneliness."

"No, thanks."

"We could just talk. About music and stuff."

"What's your name?"

"Charlotte. Gearly."

I place the name with the post I'd looked at just a short while ago and feel a fresh wave of unease. "Charlotte—"

"You never reply to my comments. I'm one of your biggest fans, and I see that you reply to other people's comments. Is it because you're afraid CeCe will be jealous?"

"CeCe doesn't get jealous."

"She's that sure of you?"

"Yes. And with reason."

She laughs a little. "Are you saying you're above temptation?"

"I'm saying I love my wife."

"Lucky girl."

"Lucky me."

"Boy, she does have you under her spell, doesn't she?"

"You need to go," I say.

"No one would have to know. If I came in for a bit, I mean."

"You're putting me in a really uncomfortable position, Charlotte. I don't want to be rude, but you're kind of crossing lines here."

"Is that right?"

"That's right."

"But don't lines only matter to the people who draw them? I don't like lines in my world. They spoil all the fun."

"Goodnight, Charlotte," I say, backing away and then heading toward the house. Hank and Patsy both throw back a bark.

Charlotte laughs. "It's nice that they want to protect you. But they don't need to do that to someone who cares about you."

I walk on without responding, not stopping until I reach the front door. I hear her car start, then pull away from the curb, engine gunning.

It takes a good bit to shake me, but nothing about what just happened feels right. I open the front door and reach for the keys to the Land Rover. I put Hank Junior and Patsy in the back seat, both of them looking at me as if I must not be aware that it's their bedtime. "We won't be gone long," I say, and reverse out of the driveway.

♪

IT ONLY TAKES a few minutes to get to Thomas and Lila's house. I swing into the driveway, turn off the engine and shut off the headlights. I send Thomas a text.

You up?

A few seconds later, he replies:

Yeah. Why?

I'm outside. All right if I come in?

Sure.

The front door opens, and Thomas walks appears. He's barefoot, and Brownie is right behind him.

I get out, opening the back door for Hank Junior and Patsy. They hop down and trot over to greet Brownie.

"Hey, man," Thomas says. "Everything all right?"

"I'm not sure."

"Lila and Lexie have already gone to bed. Come on in."

"I don't want to keep you up."

"Like I could sleep now that you've dropped that cliffhanger."

The four of us follow Thomas back in the house and into the kitchen.

"How's Lila?" I ask, as he closes the door behind us.

"Really great," he says, opening the refrigerator and pulling out a beer for both of us, handing one to me. "You look like you could use this."

All three dogs manage to curl up on Brownie's pillow in the middle of the floor. I sit down at the table and say, "The weirdest thing just happened."

"What?"

"This girl I've seen on our Facebook page was parked outside my house tonight when I took the dogs for a walk. I guess she was waiting for me."

"What did she want?"

I hesitate and then say, "To come in. She knew CeCe was away."

"Whoa."

"She's made some questionable comments on the page. I didn't take them seriously. But showing up like that — I told her she was crossing lines."

"What did she say?"

"That she doesn't believe in lines."

Thomas leans back and takes a sip of his beer. "Should you call the police?"

"And tell them what? She talked to me?"

"It was a little more than that. Waiting for you to come out of your house. That's a little creepy."

"I don't know," I say. "I don't want to get CeCe all worried about it."

"We both know what can happen when a person isn't operating on all cylinders."

I think about the shooting and the nightmare that took over our lives as a result of it. "Yeah. But what are the odds?"

"In the world we live in? I'd say pretty good."

"I'm probably making a big deal out of it."

"If anything else happens, promise you'll tell me?"

"Pinky promise," I say, reaching for a lighter note.

Thomas rolls his eyes and says, "Are you falling apart with CeCe away for a week?"

"It's lonely as heck," I say.

"Makes you wonder how we ever did without them, doesn't it?" Thomas asks.

"How'd we get so lucky?"

"I don't know," he says, shaking his head. "But we sure did, didn't we?"

♪

CeCe

I'M BEGINNING TO REALIZE there are only a few people in life you can truly be yourself with.

For me, Mama is one of those few people.

It's been too long since we've had this kind of time together, and I know I'm to blame. We're sitting on the sofa in the living room, drinking a cup of coffee and watching the eleven o'clock local news. We've covered most of our regular subjects, but the silence between us is a comfortable one in which I don't feel obligated to add unnecessary words.

But there is something I've wanted to ask her about and have been putting off, because I thought she would tell me when she was ready.

"Do you ever talk to Case, Mama?"

She takes a sip of her coffee, then sets the cup in its saucer, as if she's trying to figure out how best to answer my question. "Not in a while," she says.

"May I ask why not?"

"Honey, it's complicated."

"I'm listening," I say.

She's quiet for several seconds, and then says, "I guess at some point along the way, I started to realize that I'm just not the kind of woman a man like Case Phillips is going to stay interested in forever."

"Mama, I'm pretty sure he was crazy about you."

"And I'm pretty sure I helped him through a horrible time in his life. But it just didn't seem like it was a fairy tale that would have any chance of ending well."

"Is that how he saw it too?"

She shakes her head. "Not at the time, no. But I expect he feels differently now. You know how many women he must have after him."

"But does that matter if none of them is the one he wants?"

She considers this for a moment, and then says, "It's all water under the bridge now, honey."

"You should call him sometime, Mama. See how he's doing."

"I think that would just make it worse for us both."

"So you do still care about him?"

She starts to say something, hesitates and then finishes, "How could I not? And that's what makes me sure I did the right thing. Sometimes loving someone means you have to be willing to let them go."

I want to argue with her, but I can't. Because I know from my own life that sometimes that's exactly what you have to do in order for something to prove itself real.

♪

I CALL HOLDEN after I get in bed, needing to hear his voice before I go to sleep. He answers on the first ring.

"Hey, baby," he says.

"Hey. Were you asleep?"

"No. We just got home. Hung out with Thomas and Brownie for a bit."

"Girl talk?"

"Of a sort," he says.

"Everything all right?"

"Yeah. We just miss you like crazy."

"I miss all of you too."

"The question is who do you miss more? Me or the dogs?"

"That's hardly a fair question," I say.

"I should know better than to go there, huh?"

"You know I miss you. Especially at this time of day."

"If I start thinking about what we'd be doing right now if you were here, I'm going to be in big trouble."

"How so, sir?"

"CeCe—"

"All right," I say with a laugh. "I'll quit."

"Are you having a good visit with your mama?" he asks in an obvious change of subject.

"Yes. We had a quiet night in. It was wonderful."

"I'm sure she's missed you."

"Yeah. We need to visit her more often."

"We'll make time for it, okay?"

"That would mean a lot to me."

"I love your mama."

"And her cooking."

"How could I not?"

"I did ask her about Case tonight."

"What about him?"

"Why she stopped seeing him."

"What did she say?"

"Basically that she didn't think they had a chance of lasting, and she didn't want to put either of them through that."

"That's kind of sad."

"It is sad."

"Is she seeing anyone?"

"No. I wonder if Case is."

"I haven't heard anything about it, but that doesn't mean he's not."

"Should we talk to him?"

"About?"

"The reason Mama broke it off."

"That sounds tricky, CeCe. I'm not sure we should interfere. You do remember the first time we saw Case? In Lauren's office? Naked as they could be? He was a playboy then."

I shake my head, smiling a little. "You know he's different now."

"I think he probably really is, but your mama has a good head on her shoulders."

"It just seems like a shame for them to be apart if they love each other."

"I think we're going to have to let them figure that out."

"Her birthday is in two weeks. Why don't we have a party for her at our house?"

"And invite Case?"

"We always invite him to anything we have."

"So this would be like a coincidence?"

"They would just *happen* to be at the same party."

"Your matchmaking hat is on to stay, isn't it?" Holden says.

"I promise not to go overboard with it."

"I think I'll leave this one up to you, babe."

"I'll behave."

"Okay. Will Sunday ever get here?"

"One more day. Then I'll be home."

"I can't wait."

"Me either."

"Plan to spend the night and possibly the next day with no clothes on."

I laugh and slide down on my pillows, closing my eyes to picture his face. "Whatever for?"

He proceeds to tell me. And it's a while before we say good-night.

♪

Holden

ON SATURDAY NIGHT, Thomas and I meet Lewis Parker for dinner at the Capitol Grille at the Hermitage Hotel in downtown Nashville.

The restaurant is nearly full, a place where producers and label executives regularly meet. Lewis is waiting for us at a table in the center of the room when we arrive. He stands and shakes our hands, thanking us for taking the meeting with him.

"Well, we've heard a lot of good things about you," Thomas says as we sit down.

"Likewise," Lewis says. "Apart from your music, you guys have a nice reputation around town. Even the label couldn't say anything bad."

"We're grateful for everything that happened for us there," I say. "We've just felt we wanted more creative control and choice of direction with the music we're making."

"Understood," Lewis says, waving a waiter over. "It's a new world out there."

The waiter is a young guy who smiles when he recognizes us. He takes our drink orders before saying, "Can I just say how much I love y'all's music? It's so cool to meet you in person."

"Thanks, man," I say.

"You in the biz?" Thomas asks him.

"Trying to be," he says, humble.

"Follow your own sound," I tell him. "And just keep playing for the people who want to hear that."

"But how do you do that?" he asks, and I can tell he really wants to know. "I mean how do you find those people?"

"One listener at a time. It doesn't matter if you're playing in front of five people or five hundred, start building an email list so you have a permanent way to let them know about future shows and releases. Whether you're doing a live show or reaching them online, have a way for them to easily sign up for a free download of a song or something in exchange for their email. Keep building that list from the ground up. You'd be surprised what a thousand fans can help you do."

"Cool," he says. "I can't tell you how much I appreciate the advice. I'm Luke, by the way. Luke Matthews. Thank you so much. I'll be right back with your drinks."

Once he's out of hearing range, Lewis leans back in his chair, looking surprised. "That was amazingly generous of you."

"Not really," I say. "Everyone starts out from the same place."

"Some might consider it training up the competition."

Thomas shakes his head. "I think Holden and I both have always believed that as long as we're giving people what they want to hear, putting out music that resonates, then we'll have a place in this business, regardless of who else is in it or trying to get in it. If you're always working for your audience, and not against your competition, you've got a far better chance of sticking with people."

Lewis raises his eyebrows. "Gotta say, I haven't met many artists like you two. I've known a lot more who see it as an elbowing others out of the way kind of thing."

I shrug. "What was it the playwright Mizner told someone who wanted to be a movie star? 'Be kind to everyone on the way up; you'll meet the same people on the way down.' I guess that pretty much sums it up."

Luke returns with our drinks, and Lewis gives us his take on how he can be of help to us. He has fresh ideas, and it's clear that he's open to working outside the traditional parameters. Once he's done, he excuses himself to return a call that rang in on his phone while he was talking with us. Thomas and I take the time to make a decision.

"I like what he said," Thomas says. "I know I haven't been pulling my weight lately, buddy. You've been taking up the slack, and that takes time away from writing."

"You've been doing exactly what you need to be doing. And what I'd be doing if I were you. You have a good feeling about Lewis?"

"Yeah. And you've already checked him out. He had some pretty glowing recommendations."

"So he's hired?"

"He's hired," Thomas says.

When Lewis gets back to the table, we seal it all with a handshake, paperwork to follow tomorrow. We finish our drinks and set up a time to meet at Lewis's office. He picks up the check; we shake hands, and he leaves, assuring us we won't regret the partnership.

"Think he's right?" Thomas asks as Lewis walks out the door.

"I hope so."

"All right, man, I gotta get home. CeCe's back tomorrow?"

"Yeah, I'm picking her up at the airport."

We get up from the table, heading for the exit when a woman at the bar waves. It takes a moment for the face to register, but then I realize it's Charlotte from last night.

"Who's that?" Thomas asks.

"Let's go," I say, walking faster.

But not fast enough, because she beats us to the door. "You're not leaving so early, are you?" she asks.

She's standing between Thomas and me and the exit. "Actually, yeah," I say. "Early day tomorrow."

"When I saw you sitting over there, I couldn't believe my luck," she says. "Two nights in a row."

I'm not sure what I'm supposed to say to this, since it was clear that last night was no coincidence.

She smiles a flirtatious smile. "And now, not one, but two of you. That's crazy lucky."

"Enjoy your night, miss," Thomas says. "We've gotta be going."

"Sure I can't buy you a drink?"

"We're good," I say.

The silence becomes uncomfortable enough that she finally steps aside, a convincingly polite smile in place. "Later, then."

Neither of us says anything until we reach the parking lot where we left our vehicles.

"She's the girl from last night?" Thomas asks.

"Yeah."

"So I'm just a little creeped out."

"Hopefully, she got the message."

"Should we call the police? She seems pretty bold."

"I know. But there's nothing to accuse her of."

"You're right. But something definitely felt off."

"I'll keep an eye out for anything that seems weird."

"All right, man," Thomas says, getting in his truck. "See you tomorrow."

He pulls out ahead of me, and I'm backing out of the parking space, when I spot Charlotte in the rear camera, standing right behind the Land Rover.

I hit the brake, and she walks around to my window.

"What the hell?" I say, mad now. "I could have run over you."

"You wouldn't do that," she says, smiling as if we're having a normal conversation. "Would you like to go back in and have that drink?"

"I gotta tell you," I say, shaking my head. "This feels like it's getting out of hand."

"What? Me being polite and wanting to buy you a drink?"

"Look, Charlotte, you've got the wrong idea. I'm not interested in having a drink with you. Please don't do this again, or I'll have to call the police."

A flash of anger crosses her face, but instantly dissolves into her earlier pleasant expression. "Why would you do that? I'm one of your biggest fans. I can't imagine that there's anyone who's bought more of your music, seen more of your shows—"

"And I appreciate that. But it doesn't give you license to invade my personal life."

"Invade? Is that how you see it?"

"Yes, actually, it is."

"That's pretty ironic then. You want people to follow you, to like what you do, to tell others about it. You want us to spend our money on you but as soon as we ask for anything from you—"

"I have to go. This is getting unreasonable."

She steps back, raising a hand in the air in concession. "I don't think I'm the one who's being unreasonable here."

I raise the window and pull out of the parking lot, forcing myself not to glance in the rearview mirror. I lock my hands on the steering wheel to keep them from shaking.

♪

Charlotte

I'D LIKE TO go back in the bar and have another drink, but the place is way expensive and not somewhere I would normally pick for spending what's left of my weekly paycheck. But after following Holden here, I decided it would be worth the splurge to hang out in a place where people like him and Thomas hang out.

It was so worth it. Sitting at the bar, sipping on my twelve dollar cocktail, watching the two of them meeting with that big-wig looking guy, I felt like I was part of their world, and not just from the outside looking in.

I walk to my car. It's on the other side of the lot in a far corner where it doesn't have to suffer the comparison between its seen-better-days appearance and the Ferraris and Mercedes parked up front.

I get inside and close the door, tapping the screen on my phone and pulling up my Facebook page. I start typing.

Status: Major sighting tonight. #HoldenAshford at the Capitol Grille. That smile. That voice. #LuckyMe

I post it. And then decide to also add it to my Twitter feed as well.

I can hardly wait to get home and see what people say.

I resist the impulse to check the feed while I'm driving. It's not safe, and I'd rather let the comments build up until I'm alone in my room and can savor all the jealousy.

I stop at a drive-through and pick up some food for my dad. Two burgers, two fries, two Cokes — his regular late-night snack. I could let the ping of resentment tapping at my chest get a foothold, but all that does is get me worked up. And then I won't be able to go to sleep.

He's up when I let myself in the apartment. He's watching late night TV and sitting in the double chair, which he can barely squeeze into. I have this visual that one day, the sides will just explode in protest.

"That you, Charlotte?" he calls out.

"Yes, Daddy," I say. "I'm home."

"You're out late."

"Met up with some friends," I say, walking over to hand him the food bags.

"Anybody you planning to bring home soon?" he asks, taking the bags from me and immediately pulling out the burgers and unwrapping them.

"Not yet," I say, heading for the kitchen to pour myself a glass of water. I sip it slowly, waiting for the next question.

"You're not ashamed of your old man, are you?"

"No, Daddy. I just haven't met the right person yet."

"He'll have to be mighty special," he says around a mouthful of food, "to deserve my little girl."

Or to risk upsetting your food train, I silently add.

For a moment, I want to tell him, because I know he would never believe I could get anyone like Holden Ashford. I want to tell him that one day soon I won't have to live in this place. That Holden will love me so much that he will not want me to work or spend most of my paycheck buying food for Daddy. He'll want to hire someone to do what I've been doing since I was fourteen years old. He'll want me to have a different existence altogether. Like the one he's given CeCe. And as soon as he realizes I'm the real love of his life, and not her, that is exactly what will happen.

I can wait until then. I can't expect him to realize any of this overnight. And so until that happens, I'll keep doing what I'm doing. Working all day at the body shop I hate. Making sure Daddy's social workers continue to come in and check on him. That the nurse comes every other day to bathe him. And that I keep the refrigerator stocked with food.

I can keep doing this for as long as it takes for Holden to start loving me.

"Good night, Daddy," I say, and head for my room to check Facebook and Twitter.

♪

CeCe

MY FLIGHT LANDS in Nashville at 4:05.

I can hardly wait to get off the plane, pulling my carry-on through the tunnel that leads to the terminal.

I immediately see Holden, waiting for me off to the side of the main throng of people. He's wearing a ball cap and looking at his phone. At the sight of him, my heart thuds the way it always does when we've been apart.

I run the last few steps to him. He looks up, and a smile breaks across his face.

"Hey, baby," he says.

"Hey," I say, launching myself into his arms and kissing him with undeniable proof of how much I've missed him.

Behind us, I hear someone say, "Aren't they those singers . . . Holden and CeCe?"

"Yeah," someone else says, "Get a picture!"

Holden takes my hand and starts leading me through the airport, still kissing me as we go.

"We should keep this PG," he says.

"Okay," I say. "But only until we get home."

♪

WE DON'T EVEN make it upstairs to the bedroom before we're pulling each other's clothes off.

"What about Hank Junior and Patsy?" I ask with a giggle. "We don't want to shock them."

"They're in the back yard. They were snoozing in the sun and didn't want to come in when I left the house."

He reaches for the zipper of my dress, sliding it down slowly, deliberately. I pull his shirt from his jeans, run my hands across his back. My dress drops to the stairs, and I step out of it. I unbutton his shirt, sliding it off him. I run my hands over his well-defined arms, linger on his biceps.

23

"Do you have any idea how much I missed this?" I say, the words short and breathless.

"I'm hoping you're about to show me," he says with a smile.

"Oh, I am," I say.

We reach the top of the stairs, and it's there that he lifts me off my feet and into his arms, walking us into the bedroom, where he kicks the door closed behind us.

We fall onto the bed and roll to the middle, touching, kissing, reacquainting.

"A week," he says, "and you've reduced me to this."

"I should go away more often."

"No, you shouldn't. You definitely shouldn't."

"With this kind of welcome home, it's tempting."

"You don't need to go away to get this."

As hungry as we are for each other, Holden slows everything down, kissing me until I can't think, touching me until I can't find another breath on my own. He is my breath. My air.

We manage to get rid of the rest of our clothes, sliding them to the floor so that it's just us, the sheets cool and smooth beneath my back. He stretches my arms above my head and kisses his way down my neck, my breasts, my belly.

"Holden, please," I say.

And he doesn't make me wait another second.

♪

IT'S NEARLY TEN O'CLOCK, and we're in the kitchen eating a late dinner. Hank Junior and Patsy are still following me wherever I go, their tails wagging in happiness that I'm home. I've wondered so many times why a lonely person wouldn't have a dog. They make you feel like the center of their existence.

"Did you miss me as much as they did?" I ask Holden when he sits down at the table beside me.

"Not fair. They have the advantage of being able to wag their tail as evidence," he says, smiling.

I laugh. "Your gladness to see me was just as evident."

"Good to know. These two are tough competition."

"So tell me about the meeting with Lewis."

"Thomas and I both liked him. I think he'll be a definite asset."

"Good. I can't wait to meet him."

"He's looking forward to meeting you."

We eat in silence for a bit until I say, "Is everything all right, Holden? You seem like something's bothering you."

"Yeah," he says, reaching down to rub Patsy's head and not looking at me. "Actually, there is something I should probably tell you about."

My imagination goes into instant overdrive, and I sit back a little, saying, "What is it?"

"No big deal. It's just this girl who—"

He breaks off there, obviously struggling to find the right words.

"Girl who what, Holden?" I ask carefully.

"She was waiting outside the house the other night when I took the dogs for a walk."

"What did she want?"

"I don't know. Maybe she's just lonely or something. But she also showed up at the Grille when Thomas and I met Lewis there. She followed me out to the parking lot and wanted me to go back in for a drink with her."

"Did you?" I ask, and instantly regret it.

"Of course not," he says, surprised by the question. "CeCe."

"I'm sorry. I didn't mean it like that."

"She's just a girl who's taken the fan stuff a little too seriously."

"Holden, we know what happens when people go there."

"I know. And I'm not trying to downplay that. But I really don't think she'll show up again. I just thought you should know."

"Would you consider keeping that from me?"

He doesn't say anything for a moment, and then, "If I did, it would only be because I didn't want you to worry."

"I'm right to worry."

"I thought we'd agreed not to live our lives like that."

"I have no desire to live in fear, but a red flag is a red flag."

"I really think she's harmless, babe."

I sigh, reach across the table for his hand. "I'm sorry. I don't mean to be difficult."

"And I didn't want to upset you."

"I don't want anything to happen to you."

He slides back his chair, pats his lap, and says, "Come here."

I walk around the table, slide one leg across him so that we are face to face.

"Nothing is going to happen," he says.

I lean in and kiss him. "I just love you so much."

"I love you more," he says.

"Not possible."

"Possible."

♪

Charlotte

RATHER THAN GOING out to get Daddy's food tonight, I order two large pizzas and wait for them to be delivered. I place them on the table next to his chair and tell him I'm going to bed early.

He barely hears me, because he's already focused on the pizza, so I go in my room and close the door. I used to love the smell of pizza, but now it just sickens me. It's as if part of the effect of my father's overeating has transferred to me. He gets the weight, and I get the repulsion factor that comes with eating so much of a food that it should make you sick.

On my bed, I pick up my laptop and click into Facebook. I'm thrilled to see that there are still new responses to my post about seeing Holden and Thomas at the Capitol Grille.

> **Mandy Summers** Wow, girl. Wish I could see me some Holden Ashford. Would probably jump him on the spot.

> **Carey Bloomington** How do you rate? If I could afford the Capitol Grille, I might have a chance of running into one of those hunks.

I bask for a moment in their envy. That's what happens when you associate with people who have made it big. Everyone looks at you differently. There was a time when I thought I might have a chance to make it like that. When I had hopes of doing something with my life other than working for barely more than minimum wage and being the food delivery service for my dad. But that hasn't happened. And so the next best thing is hitching my wagon to a star that's already gleaming bright in the sky.

I click over to the Barefoot Outlook page, hoping to get a clue as to where Holden might show up next.

The photo is at the top of the feed.

> **Toni Casteen** Hey y'all – happened to be waiting for someone to get off the same plane as CeCe. Witnessed your happy reunion. Sigh.

I stare at the picture, a wave of red heat washing over me. For a moment, it fills my brain so that I can't get to another thought.

I make the photo bigger. Holden's hands are tangled in CeCe's long, blonde hair. Her head is tilted back, and he is kissing her. He's wearing a Barefoot Outlook ball cap that shadows his face. I zoom in more, and I can see that he's not into it.

Relief floods through me. He's playing the part of a happy husband. His wife is home. If he acts like he's not glad to see her, she'll get suspicious. And he doesn't want that. He has to be thinking of me while he's kissing her. Remembering our last encounter.

This is the actual truth. Regardless of what the picture implies.

I read through all the comments:

> **Morgan Miller** Y'all are so cute together.
> **Sandy Thompson** Wish I had been there to see you!
> **Mike Handy** When's the next release?
> **Katie Bartley** you two make me believe in fairy tales.

I stop reading, scroll back to the top and click on comment. I type my response without screening it.

> **Charlotte Gearly** Fairy tales are for toddlers. Do you really believe a picture like this tells the true story? If you think this is the truth, you know nothing about Holden Ashford.

I want to say more, enlighten these idiots to reality, but I don't want to risk my Facebook account, and so I force myself to close the laptop and slide it under the bed.

I turn off the lamp and curl into a ball, my knees against my chest.

She doesn't need him. She has everything. And even without him, she will have everything most people could ever dream of. Even if they aren't married anymore, there's no reason why they couldn't keep making music as a group. Thomas is married to someone else. Eventually, CeCe could be with someone else, and Holden could be with me.

He probably feels some kind of loyalty to her. But that can change.

With time. Once he starts to think about his attraction to me, whatever he feels for her will start to fade.

I can wait.

I will wait.

It will be so worth it.

♪

CeCe

I SPEND MONDAY and Tuesday catching up on life stuff. Holden is writing a lot, so he's pretty much locked himself in the studio on the other side of our back yard. When we bought the house, it included a small guest house that Holden spent a few months converting into a studio.

He loves spending time there, blocking out the world and just focusing on the music. Thomas comes over for several hours on Tuesday, and they work on a couple of songs together. I make some sandwiches and take them out around noon, ducking my head inside and saying, "I forget the secret handshake."

Thomas smiles, getting up to take the tray from me and kissing me on the cheek. "Hey, Vogue girl."

"Hardly," I say.

"You made the cover," he says.

"We'll see. They could still change their minds."

"Hey, babe," Holden says, looking up from his guitar.

"Hey. I figured y'all would forget to eat."

"Thanks," he says. "Those look great."

They take a break, and we sit around the desk, talking about what they've written this morning, songs we think are our strongest.

Holden's cell phone rings. He glances at the screen. "It's Lewis," he says and picks up.

He listens for a couple of minutes, then says, "Thanks, Lewis. I appreciate that."

When he clicks off, he looks at Thomas and me. "There's a comment on Facebook he thought I should know about."

"What is it?" I ask.

He taps the Facebook app on his phone and opens the page. Thomas and I walk around the desk so we can see. I see the picture of Holden and me at the top of the feed. He scrolls through the comments, stopping on one.

Charlotte Gearly Fairy tales are for toddlers. Do you really believe a picture like this tells the true story? If you think this is the truth, you know nothing about Holden Ashford.

A line of replies follows her comment.

Taryn Longmire you're the one who doesn't know him, chick

Michael Tyler thou shalt not covet

Ben Walker find your own guy

I stop reading. "She's the one you told me about?"

Holden nods, frowning. "Yeah. Lewis wants to keep an eye on her posts. He thinks we should block her if this continues."

"Most of the time, these things turn out to be nothing," Thomas says. "She's probably just some lonely girl who's fixated on a public figure."

"Giving the comments attention might be like adding fuel to the fire," I say. "Although I'd like to come back with 'are you serious'?"

Holden smiles a little. "We've been at this long enough to know that things like this come up. Let's not waste time or energy coming up with what-ifs."

I can see by the look on Holden's face that this bothers him. I put my arms around his neck and say, "Don't worry. I'm not worried. Y'all get back to writing."

"Are you serious?" Thomas says, and then adding a melody. "Or just delirious?"

Holden picks a few chords on the guitar. Thomas throws out another line, and then I follow. And for the next couple of hours, we sit around the desk, putting together a song the way we used to when we first formed the group.

By late afternoon, we're pretty sure we have our next single. R U Serious?

♪

CeCe

LILA AND I have a lunch date on Thursday at Demos' Restaurant in downtown Nashville. I offer to pick her up, but she says she'll meet me there.

I admit I'm a little worried about her coming alone, although Thomas assures me she's getting out and about by herself quite a bit. For the first few months after her surgery, he hovered to the point that she finally insisted he did not have to have his eyes on her twenty-four hours a day.

I understand, however, why he felt the need to.

I get to the restaurant first and ask for a table in the back. A very nice hostess with a beautiful white smile leads me through and I order iced tea while I wait. Lila appears within a few minutes, and I stand to greet her as she walks to the table.

"You look incredible," I say, reaching out to give her a hug.

She pushes her hair away from her face and says, "You're the one who looks incredible."

"Sit," I say, and she takes the chair next to me.

I feel the gazes of people around us but put my focus on Lila. "How are you?" I ask.

"I'm great," she says. "Really great."

"You look so good."

"I feel good."

"It's hard to believe you've been through what you have. You look really healthy, Lila."

"That's a compliment I truly appreciate."

The waitress comes to the table and hands us each a menu, then takes our drink order. "Be right back with that, ladies."

We open our menus, and I say, "Tell me what you're doing. You have this glow. Although that could be love."

Lila smiles. "I won't deny that. But I guess I've just been looking for ways to be good to my body."

"Like?"

"Well, you know Thomas and I went to the Hippocrates Health Institute for three weeks last month."

"And we haven't even caught up on that. Tell me."

"It's the place in West Palm Beach founded by Ann Wigmore. Their goal is to heal the body with living foods, wheatgrass, fresh juicing, raw salads and such."

"And Thomas ate those things?"

Lila laughs. "He did. For me, initially. But I think he's been convinced as well. He went out and bought us a juicer, found a local source for wheatgrass, and we're continuing with the things we learned there."

I sit back in my chair. "Wow. Well, just looking at you, it's clear that it's working."

"Thanks, CeCe. I'm just so grateful to have my health again. I feel like I need to do my best to take care of it."

"Truly," I say, "we should all feel that way. "I guess like so many things, we take it for granted until it's at risk."

Lila reaches into her purse and pulls out a piece of paper. "Lexie drew this for you at school. She put your name on it."

I open the white construction paper, and instantly smile at the colorful stick figure with a microphone in her hand. She's given me wild, yellow hair and really cool, dangling earrings. "I love it," I say. "I'll have to come over and give her a big kiss."

"She would love that."

"Is the school working well for her?"

"Incredible," Lila says. "She's just blossomed there."

"That's wonderful."

"It really is."

The waitress returns to take our orders. We both go for the Greek salad.

Once the server leaves the table, Lila says, "I'm trying to convince Thomas that it's okay for him to start touring with you guys again."

"The break has given us time to work on new music. To be honest, I think we've all benefited from it."

"But I know you need to book some shows. I want him to believe that I'm all right, but I think after what happened while he was away on the last tour, he's afraid to."

"It's easy to understand that."

"I know. But I just want life to be normal again. And that's part of who he is. I don't want to be responsible for keeping him from doing what he loves. Can you talk to him?"

"Yes. But I think Thomas might have to reach this conclusion on his own. You've both been through so much."

"We have. It's just time for him to start fully living again."

"I know I've said this to you before, Lila, but you're such a strong person. I don't know if I could have managed to get through what you've been through."

"We do it for the people we love, you know?"

"I do."

"It's not easy. It's hard for me to say this now, CeCe, because I know what kind of gift I've been given. But there were days after the surgery, when I found out what my father had done, that I just waited for my body to reject his heart. I knew it could never live inside of me. Not with everything that had happened. I was wrong though. I think of all the things that should have gone wrong, the likelihood that we would be a match, that he would be found in time for the transplant to be a possibility—I could go on and on with the list of reasons as to why it never should have worked. But the fact that it did, that my body didn't reject the heart, I guess, at some point, I just chose to accept that my life plan wasn't in my control or of my design. I want to be worthy of it. And for me, part of that is helping Thomas get back on track with his own dreams."

"Oh, Lila. The part of you that wants that for him, well, that's one of the reasons he loves you so much."

"He's changed my life. Lexie's life. I'll never be able to repay him. Encouraging him to do what he loves is the least I can do. Will you talk to him, CeCe?"

"I will," I say.

Our salads arrive, and we begin eating.

Lila takes a sip of her iced tea and says, "Thomas told me about the girl who's been following Holden around. Are you worried?"

I try to keep my voice light, but hear my own failure. "After what happened in D.C., it's hard not to worry a little."

"Should he report it to the police?"

"At this point, there wouldn't be a lot they could do."

"I guess that's true. But you should be careful. Both of you."

"We will."

"Maybe giving her attention would be the worst thing to do."

"You're probably right."

From there I deliberately change the subject to Lila's writing. She has a couple of songs she wants to play for us soon. I'm anxious to hear them.

Before we know it, nearly two hours have passed, and Lila says, "I have to pick up Lexie. Better get going."

"Thanks for meeting me," I say. "Girl talk always does me good."

"Me too," she says.

"I'll wait for the check," I say. "You get going. I know you don't want to be late."

"Only if you let me get it next time?"

"Deal."

We hug each other bye, and she turns at the front door to wave before disappearing onto the street.

The waitress brings over the check. I'm adding the tip to the credit card receipt when someone stops at the table. I look up to find a young woman smiling at me. She's wearing a stocking cap and sunglasses.

"Hi," she says. "You're CeCe Ashford?"

"Yes," I say, sliding my card into my wallet.

"I'm such a fan," she says. "I was wondering if you would mind signing something for me."

"Sure," I say, smiling at her. "And thank you for the kind words."

She slides into the chair where Lila had been sitting. I'm a little surprised, but wait while she fishes through her purse for a notebook. She hands it to me.

"Just anything you want to write," she says.

I sign my name and add a musical note to the side, handing it back to her.

I start to stand, saying, "I'm afraid I really have to be going."

She puts a hand on my arm to stop me. "Could I just ask you a few questions?"

I hesitate, not wanting to be rude, but at the same time, feeling as if something isn't quite right. I ease back onto the chair and say, "I only have a minute or two."

"Okay," she says. "Thank you so much."

I'm thinking she's going to ask about getting into the music business. It's something I get asked on a regular basis.

"How did you make him fall in love with you?"

"I'm sorry?"

"Holden. What did you do that made him love you?"

I sit back in my chair and stare at her for a long moment, trying to decide how to respond. "Are you the one who came to see my husband the other night?"

"I did," she says. "We had a really nice conversation."

"I'm afraid you're confused," I say.

"How so?" she asks, looking genuinely puzzled.

"Coming to our house and catching him off guard doesn't translate to having a nice conversation. In his opinion or mine."

"He seemed to enjoy it."

"I want to be nice to you. But you need to know that what you're doing is not okay with Holden, and it's not okay with me."

"CeCe," she says, as if we've known each other forever, "you and I both know that famous people get tired of each other eventually. You're both people who like to have the complete focus of the spotlight, and there will come a point when one of you gets tired of sharing it. Starts to resent. And resentment erodes love. It would actually be a kindness for you to end your marriage to Holden before that starts to happen. Or has it already?"

I scoot my chair away from the table and stand up. I look her directly in the eyes and say, "Do not come near me again, Charlotte. Do not contact my husband again. In any way, shape, or form. In person or online. Am I clear?"

"I can't make that promise, CeCe. Like you, I love him. Can you promise never to see him again?"

It occurs to me in that moment that I am not speaking to a rational person. And so I say nothing further, but turn around and walk quickly out of the restaurant.

♪

Holden

I KNOW SOMETHING is wrong as soon as she walks in the door.

Her face is pale, and she doesn't smile at me when I kiss her hello.

"What's wrong, babe?" I ask, suddenly worried.

She puts her purse and keys on the foyer table and says, "I had a run-in with Charlotte."

"Who?" I ask and then instantly connect the name. "What do you mean?"

"When Lila left Demos', she came over to my table and sat down."

"What did she say?"

"That she loves you. And she's willing to wait until we get tired of each other."

"What the hell?" I ask, anger lighting me up from the inside. "Is she for real?"

"Unfortunately," she says, walking into the kitchen where Hank and Patsy greet her with wagging tails.

She squats down to rub their heads and give them each a kiss on their ears. When she stands back up, she looks at me with worried eyes. "Holden, she really believed what she was saying."

"We need to call the police."

"I'm not sure we should."

"I don't think we have a choice. Maybe if they go and talk to her, she'll realize she can't go where she's going."

"If you think it's the right thing to do," she says, looking uncertain.

I spend the next hour on the phone in my office, starting first with our lawyer, Mitchell Harvey. He agrees that we need to report each of the incidents so that there's a record of them in case things go further. He offers to call a detective for us, and within an hour-and-a-half, he is knocking at our front door.

"Mr. Ashford?"

"Yes," I say.

"I'm Detective Gary Milner with the Metropolitan Nashville Police Department. Mitchell Harvey asked me to stop by."

"Please, come in," I say.

He follows me into the kitchen. I introduce him to CeCe. Hank and Patsy don't bother getting off their pillows, as if they realize right off the bat he's one of the good guys.

"Have a seat, please," I say, offering him a chair at the table. "This is my wife, CeCe."

"Hello," she says, taking the seat beside me.

"It's really nice to meet you both," he says. "Can you tell me what's been going on?"

"At this point, it's probably not a big deal, but I guess I'm concerned that it could be. This girl—young woman—has started to show up out of the blue. She acts as if we know each other. She was waiting at the end of the street a few nights ago, when I took the dogs out for a walk."

He pulls a notepad and pen from his pocket and starts writing on it. "And you're sure she was actually waiting for you."

"There was no one else around, and it was after eleven. I'm sure."

"I'm not questioning the truth of what you're saying. But I do want to be sure about your perception of her intent."

"Okay," I say.

"What did she say that night?"

"Mostly small talk. But I don't know, it's like she ignores boundaries that other people are aware of being there."

"Was that the only time she's approached you?"

"No. She was at a restaurant where I met a friend the next night. It wasn't a coincidence."

"Did she threaten you?"

"No," I say.

"What did she indicate was her reason for being there?"

"She said she'd like to buy me a drink."

"Did you accept?"

"No. I left the restaurant, but as I started to back out of my parking space, I saw her standing right behind my vehicle. I could have hit her. It was like that never occurred to her. When I told her if she kept following me, I would have to call the police, she got angry and said something about how we want people to spend their money on us, follow us on social media and such, but don't want to give anything back."

"And then today," CeCe says, "she approached me at a restaurant."

"Was her manner threatening?" the detective asks.

"No. I didn't realize who she was at first. She asked for an autograph."

"Did you give her one?"

"Yes, and then she asked me how I made Holden fall in love with me. It was like she was asking me for the recipe to my favorite apple pie or something."

"What else did she say?"

"That famous people always get tired of each other and resentments build up. That we'll be over each other before long. And she loves him."

The detective's expression remains neutral throughout each of these revelations, but then I guess he hears stuff like this all the time. "Do you think she's dangerous?" I ask.

He looks up at me, and I can see he wants to be straight with us. "Most likely not. It's usually a man who takes stalker behavior to a level of violence. With women, it tends to be more intimidation and threat than actual violence. Which, I'm afraid to say, makes it more difficult to charge them with anything."

"So what do we do?" CeCe asks, clearly frustrated.

"I'll do a background check, get whatever information about her I can find and then pay her a visit. Sometimes, as soon as the police become involved in a situation, the stalker will stop what she's doing."

"And what if she doesn't?" I ask.

"Then we'll increase the pressure from our side of the fence and wait for her to do something we can actually arrest her for."

CeCe throws up her hands. "So we have to sit back and hope she doesn't do something horrible?"

"I realize how unsettling this can be, ma'am," he says, his expression not unsympathetic, "but try to go on with your lives and not give this too much thought. We live in a town full of famous people. I see this kind of thing on a fairly regular basis. Most cases fizzle out on their own. The real damage comes from the fear that can take over your life, if you're not careful."

"That's easier said than done," CeCe says.

"I'm not denying that. But giving in to fear gives her power. And sometimes, that's exactly what a person like this is looking for."

He asks for some basic information then, links to all of our social media accounts, and any upcoming public appearances. When he stands to leave, he shakes our hands and says, "I'll be thorough with this. Just because I'm advising you to get on with your lives doesn't mean I'm not taking it seriously."

"Thank you," CeCe says, relief in her voice.

I follow him outside, closing the front door behind me, before I say, "I really appreciate you coming out. And just so you know, I'm not too concerned about my ability to deal with this woman. But when she approaches my wife, that's another thing altogether."

"I understand," he says. "I'd feel the same way."

"You have my cell number. Please call me if you learn anything that would be helpful."

"I certainly will," he says, walking to the unmarked blue sedan and getting inside.

I stand there for a minute or more after he pulls away, hoping he meant what he said.

♪

Charlotte

I GO BACK and forth between hating my dad for what he has become and pitying him for the place he is in.

It started when I was ten. He lost his job when the textile factory he had worked for since he got out of high school went out of business. My mom still had her job as a receptionist for a dentist's office, and so we were able to make ends meet, while my dad stayed home and looked for work. But none of the interviews ever panned out, and he sent out fewer and fewer applications, until it became clear he was no longer looking at anything other than the TV all day.

Somewhere in the middle of all that, he began eating more. Mostly fast food. Asking Mom to pick up some on the way home from work. Calling out for pizza as often as three times a day.

And he began to gain weight. Ten pounds. Then twenty. Thirty-five. At the end of his first year of being unemployed, he had gained one hundred and twenty-seven pounds.

My mom began to complain. She was spending every extra penny she made on food. Dad's unemployment checks weren't covering it. At some point, those checks ran out, because he was no longer actively looking for a job.

Mom stuck with him for just over two years before she'd reached the point of no longer being able to tolerate the life we were living. She woke me up early one morning, sitting on the edge of my bed, and whispering, "I'm leaving, Charlotte. Pack whatever you can in your suitcase. I want to be gone before he wakes up."

"What?" I had asked, rubbing my eyes to focus. "Where are we going?"

"I don't know yet. Just away from here."

"You mean leave Daddy here by himself?"

"He's a grown man, Charlotte. It's time he started acting like one."

"But he can't really take care of himself right now." By then, he was three hundred plus pounds overweight. He had ordered a double-width chair and spent most of his time in it. Even sleeping there at night.

"We can't throw our lives away just because that's what he's chosen to do with his."

"But I thought you loved him."

"He's not the same man I married."

As a twelve year old, I didn't really know what to make of this statement. My dad had a problem, like a sickness. "I can't leave him here alone."

"Charlotte, if you don't come with me, you'll regret it someday."

"Who'll take care of him though?"

"He'll take care of himself. He'll find a way."

I wanted to go. More than I wanted my next breath. But I just couldn't. I pictured my dad sitting in that chair, not able to even get up and go to the bathroom without someone helping him, and I just couldn't.

But she left anyway. Just like she said she would. Disappearing from our apartment with a single suitcase. I watched from my bedroom window as she got in the car and pulled out of the parking lot without once looking back.

It's days like today when I'm pretty sure I should have left with her. It's Saturday, and since I'm not working, I spend the morning online, Googling Holden and rereading the articles I've already read about him multiple times. There's nothing new about him on the Facebook page. Just a picture of CeCe's dog that someone posted after seeing her running with him in Shelby Park. He's as lean and fit-looking as she is.

I stand up from my desk, look at myself in the full-length mirror attached to my bathroom door. Should I start running? Is my stomach starting to poke out a bit?

I decide that yes, it is, and open a drawer in my dresser to rifle through some shorts and T-shirts I haven't used in a while. I find a pair similar in color to the ones CeCe had on in the picture. I don't have a T-shirt that looks anything like hers, but pull out one that will have to do. I look at the picture again to see how she's wearing her hair, then attempt a version of her ponytail.

Her hair is thicker than mine, but I decide I've done a passable comparison. I grab my phone and some earbuds and walk through the living room, calling out, "I'm going for a run, Dad. Be back in a little while."

"Since when do you run?" he asks.

"Since today," I answer back, sharper than intended.

"Good for you," he says. "If you happen to run by the KFC, how about picking up a bucket of chicken and an order of biscuits?"

I start to argue, tell him how he really shouldn't eat that, but how many times have I done exactly that? How many times did it do any good? It would only mean that he would eventually wear me down, and I would end up going out for something later.

I walk back into the bedroom, grab my credit card from my wallet, and retrace my steps. He's so engrossed in the game show on TV that he doesn't notice me leave.

I tell myself that he's sick, that what's wrong with him is no different than some other kind of disease that prevented him from working or going out and getting his own food.

Even so, as soon as I hit the sidewalk, I take off at a pace I can't maintain for long, my shoes pounding hard on the concrete. With each step, I try to release some of the coil of anger inside me. But my side starts to hurt before I ever reach the KFC, and when I start to walk, it is still there, wound tight, awaiting release.

♪

WHEN I GET back to the apartment forty-five minutes later, a bucket of chicken in one arm, a bag of biscuits in the other, I notice a blue sedan parked near the stairwell. Just as I start to walk by, the door opens, and a man gets out.

He's dressed in jeans and a dark blazer, a gray T-shirt and black-frame sunglasses. He smiles at me and says, "Hello. Are you Charlotte Gearly?"

"Yes," I say, surprised.

He eyes the KFC bucket and says, "Worked up an appetite on that run, huh?"

Heat floods my face. "Ah, no. It's actually not for me."

"I'm Detective Milner with the Metropolitan Nashville Police

Department. Is there somewhere we could speak for a few minutes in private?"

"Regarding what?" I ask.

"I just have a few questions for you, Miss Gearly."

"How do you know it's Miss?"

"Is it?"

I start to say no, but he's holding his badge, so I nod and say, "Yes. My dad is at home."

"That's not a problem for me."

I lead the way up the stairs, opening the apartment door with my key and leading him through to the kitchen where I set the chicken and biscuits on the counter. The TV is blaring from the living room and through the wall cut out, I can see my dad asleep in his chair. I'm surprised the smell of the chicken hasn't woken him up.

I watch the detective's face as he glances at him, his eyes widening a bit. I'm guessing he's figured out who the food was for.

"Have a seat, detective," I say, waving a hand at one of the chairs at our small table.

He sits, and I take the chair across from him. "What is this about?" I ask.

He pulls a notepad from his pocket and flips through a few pages. "I received a call from Holden and CeCe Ashford about some encounters they've had with you, Miss Gearly."

"Encounters?"

"Yes. Apparently, you waited for Mr. Ashford outside his house one evening, approached him at a bar the following night, and also approached his wife at a restaurant a couple of days later. Is that true?"

"Yes. Is that illegal?"

"No. Not at this point. But your behavior has apparently made them both uncomfortable."

"You know, Mr. Milner, there's something I don't understand about celebrities. They want the world to adore them, enough in fact to spend their hard-earned money on them, but they don't want the great unwashed to get too close, invade their inner circle. Heaven forbid, force them into a conversation with one of the fans they've worked so hard to cultivate."

"I'm not here to argue that point of view with you, Miss Gearly. But I am here to tell you that there is a line of what is acceptable and what isn't."

"And they're saying I've crossed that line."

"Yes."

"Who said that? CeCe?"

"Miss Gearly, the complaint was lodged by Mr. Ashford. For your own sake, I am advising you not to approach either one of them again."

"Wow," I say, sitting back in my chair. "Does that mean I should stop buying their music too?"

"If you like."

"Is that all, detective?"

He pushes back his seat and stands. "For now, yes. I hope we won't have to meet for this reason again."

I stand up and fold my arms across my chest. "I'm sure you can find your own way to the door."

"Good-bye," he says and walks out.

I stand for a few moments after I hear the door click, my face suffused with heat. How dare she? That spoiled bitch. She's married to him, and she can't stand sharing him even in conversation.

"Charlotte?"

"Yes, Dad?" I say, managing to keep my voice even.

"Come in here, please."

I walk into the living room, stopping in front of his oversize chair. "What is it?"

"I heard the conversation."

"I thought you were asleep."

"I wasn't deliberately eavesdropping. I didn't want to embarrass you—"

"Oh, you thought me knowing that you heard what he was saying would embarrass me? I think what would embarrass me is him seeing you."

He glances away, not letting himself meet my gaze, and then, in a low voice, says, "Charlotte. Why are you doing such a thing?"

"I'm not doing anything wrong."

"It sounds like you're stalking a married man."

"Stalking?!? Are you serious? I'm in love with him. And pretty soon, he will feel the same about me. How is that stalking?"

He looks at me for a long time before saying anything else, and then, finally, "Surely, you can see that's not the case."

"If you're implying that I'm out of touch with reality, I have no idea how you could expect me to accept your point of view. Look at you, you have no idea what reality is. So I will tell you. Reality is the fact that you are going to die in that chair. Reality is that you are eating yourself closer to your grave with every bite of food you take. Reality is you have made me your accomplice."

I stomp into the kitchen, grab the bucket of chicken and bag of biscuits, stomp back and drop them onto the tray in front of his chair. "Here, Dad. Here's your reality. Leave mine alone, okay?"

I go to my room and slam the door.

♪

CeCe

OVER THE NEXT few days, I try to put the incident with Charlotte Gearly out of my mind.

There are no posts on Facebook, and she doesn't appear in front of either me or Holden when we venture out in public. We go to Whole Foods one afternoon, and I keep expecting her to round the corner every time we head down a new aisle.

"You can't keep worrying about her," Holden says, pulling a bag of Hank and Patsy's favorite treats from the shelf and dropping it in the cart. "Detective Milner said he talked to her. And we haven't heard anything from her since. Let's put it behind us."

"I know you're right," I say. "I don't know why she has me so spooked."

Holden stops the cart and loops an arm around my waist. "I do. But neither one of us wants to live in fear of what someone might or might not do. That just makes us prisoners in our own lives."

"I'll try harder."

"We need to get your mind on something else. What about the birthday party for your mom?"

"I need to get on it."

"Then let's do it. We'll go home, work on the list, call a caterer, book your mom's flight and get everything lined up."

I slide my arms around his neck and kiss him with all the love I feel for him. "Are you for real?"

"Want me to prove it?"

"I do."

"I'll put that on the list of things to do when we get home," he says, tickling me.

I laugh and take off with the cart.

"You can run, little girl, but you can't hide."

♪

WORRY IS A cancer of sort.

I remember reading something where Winston Churchill said when

49

he thought about his own worries, he remembered the story of the old man on his deathbed who said that he'd had a lot of trouble in his life, but most of it never actually happened.

I'm lying awake, Holden asleep beside me, and my mind is projecting all sorts of what-ifs about Charlotte Gearly. What if she doesn't stop? What if she does something crazy like what happened to us in DC?

I get out of bed and go downstairs, Hank Junior and Patsy padding along behind, groggy with being woken up in the middle of the night. In the kitchen, I open the door and let them out in the backyard.

It's only three-thirty, but I start a pot of coffee, because I know I'm not going back to sleep. When my mind is this awake, it's a useless endeavor.

Somehow, I have to get a handle on my own fears. I think about the months after the shooting and how powerless I felt in my own life. How I never want to feel like that again.

Once the kettle whistles, I add some coffee to a silver French press pot and then pour in the water. I let Hank and Patsy back inside, and they settle onto their pillow in the middle of the floor.

I keep a journal and pen in a kitchen drawer, and I pull it out now, sitting down at the table and opening it to a blank page.

Journaling is something I started doing after the shooting. Just jotting down every fragment of thought I can download from my brain. It helped me come to terms with some of what had happened to us. I start to write now.

> *fear, living behind walls, what if she doesn't stop, want to live with a peaceful mind, part of being in the public eye, asked for this kind of exposure, can there be a balance, am I giving her power, none of what I'm thinking is likely to ever happen, life is a combination of getting what you want and realizing everything comes with a down side, love music, love what we do, is it worth the down side, need to feel safe in my life*

I don't stop writing until I've emptied every thought I can possibly funnel through my pen. I sit back then and read what I've written. Just seeing it all there on paper makes me feel a little better. Everyone worries about something. Health, money, losing a loved one, whether we're making good choices in our lives or not.

I think about Lila and everything she's been through in the past year. Things that could still happen with her heart. But it's clear that she's chosen not to let those worries dictate how she lives each day.

Maybe it's true that if we do give in to worrying about what might happen, it's almost as if it has. We live the fear in our minds.

I put down my pen and close the journal. I'm not going to be a victim of fear. I'm not going to give another person this kind of control over my life.

Living is about doing. Not dwelling. Moving ahead with the things that make being here meaningful. Right now, that's what I need to lose myself in. Mama has a birthday coming up. And she deserves a party.

I open the journal to a blank page and start making a list of things to do and people to invite.

♪

A WHILE LATER, I slide back into bed, wrapping my arms around Holden's shoulders and kissing his neck.

"Umm," he says, coming awake beside me. "What time is it?"

"Early," I say. "Sorry."

"You okay?"

"Yeah. Just up thinking."

He turns to face me. "Uh-oh. Not good."

"Actually, this time, I think it is. I've talked myself into some perspective on the Charlotte thing."

"Baby," he says. "I wish I knew how—"

"It's okay," I say, putting a finger to his lips. "I'm going to focus on the good stuff. Mama's party, first off. And there's something else Lila asked me to do for her."

"What?"

"She wants me to talk to Thomas about kind of the same thing. Putting fear aside and starting to do what he loves again. Performing."

"Yeah. I think he's afraid if he leaves for any length of time, something might happen."

"And I understand. But you know, our worries can make us put up bars around ourselves in the hope of preventing something from happening. Those bars don't work though, and we just end up imprisoning ourselves in our own lives."

"True," he says, running his hand across my hair. "Are you going to talk to him?"

"Maybe I'll see if he'll meet me at the gym this morning."

"Sounds good." He pulls me up snug against him. "Now that we're both wide awake, and it's not really time to get up yet, what do you think we should do?"

I smile and kiss his chin. "I don't know. Got any ideas."

"A couple."

"I'm listening," I say.

"They don't require talking."

"Oh. My favorite kind."

♪

WE MEET IN THE weight room at ten o'clock.

The gym is a small club downtown. Members are mostly people in the music industry, so no one pays much attention to either me or Thomas when we find a spot and start rotating sets.

Thomas spots me on the chest press, looking down at me and saying, "I know I'm here for a reason."

I complete the twelve reps, and he helps me place the bar back on the rack. I sit up and admit, "Lila asked me to talk to you about getting back to regular life."

Thomas adds weights to each end of the bar, takes his place on the bench before saying, "If I ever thought I knew what the definition of that was, I'm pretty sure I was wrong."

"What do you mean?"

He does fifteen reps with the heavy weight before answering. He sits up and says, "I don't know, CeCe. I guess I used to think I pretty much knew what was around the next corner. What I know for sure now is that we have no idea what is ahead for us. So I just want to hold onto what I know really matters in my life."

"I understand. But your music is part of who you are. And I think Lila wants to see you living that part of your life too."

He looks down at his hands, clenching and unclenching them. "I'm scared to leave her, CeCe."

"I know," I say, sitting down next to him on the bench. "And who wouldn't understand that? But I was thinking this morning about fear and worry and this whole Charlotte mess. And how when we let those things determine what we do, we're conceding to their power over us. I guess to really live life, we have to fight back. Not let ourselves get locked up in a closet of our own making."

"Is that what you think I'm doing?"

"I think you're scared to death of losing the woman you love, but she's doing great, Thomas. Maybe she just wants you to see that and believe in it."

He doesn't say anything for a good bit. We know each other so well that I don't wonder if I've offended him or overstepped my boundaries.

"So what are y'all thinking for a tour?" he asks after a bit.

"Holden says Lewis has a couple of plans he wants to show us. Ultimately, it will be our call."

"Set up the meeting," he says. "I'll be there."

"Really?" I ask, surprised.

"The truth is Lila fell in love with a singer. Not a house husband. It's a good thing because I really suck at that."

I laugh, hugging him. "I love you."

"I love you too."

♪

Holden

CECE THROWS HERSELF headfirst into planning her mama's birthday party. We haven't given ourselves a lot of time to get it together, so we spend a few days working on little else.

We send out over a hundred invitations, planning to have the party at our house with a catered dinner and a band for dancing. We're looking at a menu one afternoon in the kitchen when CeCe says, "Do you think Case will come?"

"If he's in town, I would think so," I say.

"I don't know how awkward things are with him and Mama. What if he brings a date?"

"I don't think he would do that."

"But what if he did?"

"Want me to call him?"

"Is that a bad idea?"

"I can just ask if he's coming."

CeCe slips her arms around my neck, kisses me softly. "You're too good to me."

"I do have some payback arrangements in mind."

"You usually do," I say.

"Would you like to cash in?"

"I don't like to let debts pile up."

"Me either."

So we go upstairs.

♪

THE NEXT MORNING, I drive over to Thomas's house, and we spend a few hours fine-tuning a couple of songs. It's lunchtime when we're done. I stop to get gas on the way home, pulling up to the pump, and waiting for the tank to fill.

"Hey, Holden."

I turn, and it's Charlotte, smiling an uncertain smile. "Hey," I say, trying to keep my voice neutral.

"Small world, isn't it?"

"Is it?" I ask, doubting this is a coincidence.

"How are you?"

"Charlotte, you have to stop this."

"What? Being polite to you?"

"Appearing out of nowhere."

"Was it your idea to have that detective come and see me, or was it CeCe's?"

"It was my idea," I say.

"I don't believe that."

"It's true."

"She's very possessive of you. I don't guess I can blame her, but it makes her a little paranoid, I think."

"Do you hear yourself? There's nothing normal about what you're saying."

"Those are just my observations."

The gas nozzle clicks, and I pull it out of the tank, anxious to leave. "I have to go," I say.

She puts a hand on my arm. "If you need to keep her in the picture for a while, I'm okay with that. We can see each other without her knowing it."

I step back with both my hands in the air, because I honestly don't trust myself not to shove her away from me. "Listen. You and I are not seeing each other. We are not ever going to see each other. I am married. I love my wife. I don't want you to come near me again. Am I clear?"

She stares at me, smiling as if I've said nothing at all. "Your loyalty is a very appealing trait. Maybe misguided, but appealing. You will see her differently one day. It happens in every marriage. And when it does, I'll be here for you."

I decide then that I'm better off not saying another word. I get in the Land Rover and pull away from the gas station, slamming my right palm against the steering wheel.

There's crazy. And there's Charlotte.

♪

Charlotte

HE SAID HE was the one who called the police, but I don't believe him.

He's protecting her.

At some point in our life together, I know I will appreciate this about him. It truly is an admirable quality.

I'm sure she's the one who brought about my visit from Detective Milner. Does she really think she can change the way I feel about Holden by trying to scare me off with thin threats, when I haven't done anything illegal?

It's easy to see how a girl like CeCe could become overconfident. By most definitions, she has the world at her feet. But she doesn't scare me. I'm not intimidated by her success or her beauty. Because I know where Holden's heart really is. Who he writes his songs for. It's me. Not her.

She can call the police as many times as she wants to. It won't change any of that.

However, I am human, and maybe it's time to teach her a little lesson.

♪

CeCe

I LET HANK AND PATSY out in the backyard after lunch. It's a mild day, and they like to snooze on their outdoor pillows in the sunshine, so I decide to leave them out for a bit.

Holden is on the phone with Lewis, trying to work out a sixty-day tour. I have a hair appointment in thirty minutes and leave a note for Holden on the kitchen counter, asking him to let Hank and Patsy in when he's off the phone.

The salon is twenty minutes from our house, and I give Mama a quick call to make sure she and Aunt Vera have their tickets for the flight to Nashville. She assures me everything is all set and not to worry.

I make it to the appointment with a couple of minutes to spare. Daisy Clemmons, the pretty young owner of the salon, has just led me to the shampoo sink when my phone buzzes. I glance at the screen. There's a text from Holden.

Did you take Hank with you? He's not in the yard.

My stomach takes a nose dive. "I'm sorry, Daisy. I need to make a quick call."

"No problem," she says. "You can use my office if you'd like. Follow me."

She opens the door. I step inside and she closes it behind me. I tap on Holden's number, wait for him to answer, my heart pounding.

"Hey," he says. "Do you have him?"

"No. Was Patsy in the yard?"

"Yes."

"Where is he? He couldn't possibly jump the fence. It's six feet high."

"I know, but I've looked everywhere for him."

"Did you check the gate at the back?"

"It's closed. But the padlock wasn't on it."

"It's supposed to be."

59

"I know."

"Oh, Holden," I say, my voice breaking in half. "Do you think someone took him?"

"Babe, I don't know. But it's possible."

"Hank." I can't say anything else because I start to cry.

♪

Charlotte

MY CAR IS small, and he takes up most of the backseat.

He's stretched out with his head on his paws, and every time I glance back at him, I can see he's worried about where I'm taking him.

It really wasn't hard to get through the gate. A pair of lock cutters from Walmart, and the padlock snapped in half.

I've seen pictures of both the dogs on Facebook, so I knew which one was CeCe's. Hank Junior. I say his name, and he looks up at me.

"I'm sorry to have to do this to you, fella," I say. "It's not anything that you've done. But I think your mama needs to know what it feels like to be threatened with losing something she loves."

I considered dropping him off on the other side of the city, but then he would have a decent chance of being picked up by the local animal control and returned home. And so I decided to drive him a couple of hours away from Nashville, find a spot somewhere out in the boonies to dump him.

"It won't be so bad. Maybe a family on a farm will take you in. You're probably tired of being a city dog, anyway."

It occurs to me an hour or so down the road that he might need to go potty, and I sure don't want him doing that in my car. I find a place to pull over and reach for the leash I had also bought at Wal-mart, hooking it to his collar and waiting for him to jump out.

I walk him over to a grassy spot, but he's not interested in peeing, looking up at me with his still worried eyes. "Are you sure you don't have to go? All right. Come on, then. Let's get you down the road a bit, so you can start looking for your new life."

♪

CeCe

AS SOON AS I hang up with Holden, I remember the GPS app we had purchased for Hank Junior and Patsy last year when a friend told us about it. She had lost her dog while on vacation in Atlanta, and the GPS tag on his collar had helped her find him in no time.

I tap into the app, login and click on Hank's name. After a few seconds, a map comes up on the screen, and a blinking red light indicates he's about an hour from here on I-40.

I call Holden back and tell him what I've found. "He couldn't have gotten that far on his own," I say. "Someone took him."

"We can track him as long as the GPS signal is working."

We decide on the closest place for us to meet up by the Interstate—a Starbucks where I will leave my car. Holden is already there, waiting for me when I pull in. I get out and jump in the Rover, and we take off.

I plug my phone into the charger just to make sure we don't lose the connection.

"Do you think it's her?" I ask him once we're on the Interstate.

"I honestly can't imagine that she would go there after everything that's been said, but it's possible."

"What if she hurts him?" I can barely get the question out.

"Let's not go there, hon. We'll do everything we can to get to him."

Holden pushes the speed limit, passing cars whenever he can. The GPS still indicates he's on I-40 about an hour and ten minutes ahead of us.

I try not to think about all the things that could happen to him. But I can't stop myself, and tears run down my face.

Holden reaches over to take my hand, squeezing hard. "We've been here one other time, remember? And we found him. We'll find him again, okay?"

I nod, biting my lip and trying not to cry.

Holden stares straight ahead for a few moments, and then says, "I saw her earlier today."

"Charlotte?" I ask, surprised.

"Yes. She was at the gas station when I stopped after leaving Thomas's."

"What did she say?"

"A lot of stuff that didn't make any sense."

"Why didn't you tell me?"

"I didn't want you to worry."

"And now she's taken Hank." I don't mean for it to sound accusing, but it does.

"I'm sorry, CeCe. I'm really sorry."

♪

Charlotte

TWO HOURS FROM Nashville seems far enough.

I take an exit off the Interstate that doesn't seem to have much going for it. I turn right and follow the two-lane road a few miles until I see a place to pull off. A gravel road runs alongside a green field of what looks like wheat.

"Maybe that farmer I told you about lives back there somewhere." I get out of the car and open the back door. "Come on. You can go check. Maybe that will be your new home."

The dog hops out, reluctant, ducking his head a little as I bend down to remove his collar, tossing it into the field just beyond us. "It's nothing personal, boy. I'm not really doing this to you. You're kind of just the fallout, I guess."

He looks up at me, and I swear, if I didn't know better, I would think he understood every word. "Go on now," I say, waving my hands. "Get away from the road. You don't want to get hit by a car."

He doesn't move, so I increase my hand waving until he trots off a bit, turning to look back at me with his worried expression.

"You'll be fine," I say, and then raising my voice, "Go on!"

This time, he tucks his tail and starts to run, not looking back.

I get in the car, closing the door and hooking my seat belt. I feel a little guilty for deserting him here, but then again, I had originally thought about poisoning him in CeCe's backyard. This is much kinder, for him, anyway. I'm sure CeCe will always wonder if he's dead or alive. But I'll know that most likely, he is just fine. And as long as I know it, that's all that counts.

♪

Holden

I'M NOT GOOD at feeling out of control. And that's exactly how I feel right now.

I've learned enough about life already to know that we aren't in control of much in this world. But I have come to believe that we take care of our own and, to the best of our ability, protect them.

I can feel CeCe's pain as if it is being released from her in waves. It rolls over me, like surf after a storm, and I struggle for footing, aware that we have to find Hank Junior.

"Should we call the police, Holden?"

"As long as we have the GPS signal, I think we should keep going."

"Would she hurt him?"

"I can't imagine that she would."

"Why would she do this?"

"For now, let's not assume that she did. People steal dogs."

"But Patsy was out there too."

"Maybe she wouldn't come to the person. Hank is a friendly guy."

CeCe holds up her phone, pointing to the screen. "The signal is staying in one place. Here."

I glance at it and say, "How far away?"

"Forty minutes."

I drive way faster than I should, and we reach the road indicated by the GPS in thirty-two minutes. It's a small gravel road, and I slow the Land Rover as we get closer to the signal. I turn in, cut the engine and open the door to jump out.

The area is several miles off the Interstate, little here but cows and pasture land as far as you can see.

CeCe gets out on her side, and we both start calling for Hank. We call and call, but there's no sign of him.

"The signal still indicates this spot," CeCe says. "Could his collar be around here somewhere?"

"It might be," I say, and start walking through the high grass on one side of the road. CeCe takes the other, and we search until I hear her call my name.

"I found it!" she says.

I turn around to see her holding the collar up in the air. She is at once elated and crestfallen. "He might not be anywhere near here," she says. "They could have thrown the collar out the window if they realized it had a tracker."

I walk over and put my arms around her. "Let's go on the assumption that he's somewhere nearby. We'll see where this road goes and stop at every house to ask if anyone has seen him."

CeCe presses the collar to her chest, nodding, tears sliding down her cheeks.

♪

CeCe

IT'S AN ABSOLUTELY horrible feeling to lose a dog.

Once they're out of your protection, they can't tell anyone that they're lost. If they're not wearing a collar, they can be picked up by animal control and taken to the pound as a stray.

I keep thinking about the other time that Holden and I searched for Hank and ended up finding him at the county shelter in Nashville. Seeing him there behind that cage door, where he would wait out his allotted time had nearly broken me. I knew that if we hadn't found him, he would have been led from that kennel to a room where his life would have been ended, as if he had never mattered to anyone at all.

Just the thought that he could be in that same situation again is more than I can let myself consider.

We drive down the small gravel road, windows lowered, both of us calling his name out the window. When we come to a farmhouse on the right, Holden stops, and I get out, knocking on the door.

An older woman with white hair and a questioning smile asks if she can help me. I tell her we're looking for our dog, and she says she hasn't seen him. I give her my cell number in case she does.

We pass four more houses, and I repeat the same questions at each one. No one has seen him.

We're a mile off the main road, when Holden says, "CeCe, there he is."

Hank Junior is sitting at the base of a large oak tree. When he spots us, he stands up and starts wagging his tail so hard it's a blur.

"Oh, my gosh!" I say, jumping out before Holden has fully stopped the Land Rover and running to Hank.

He leaps at me, and I swear if he could wrap his front legs around me, he would. I start to cry, great heaving sobs that stop me from doing anything except dropping to my knees and hugging him as tightly as I can.

He licks my face nonstop, his gratitude undeniable. Holden drops down beside the two of us, and I can feel his relief like something I could actually touch. He puts his arms around both of us, and we just sit there on the side of a country road, thankful beyond any words we have the ability to express.

♪

Holden

CECE SITS IN the back with Hank Junior on the return drive to Nashville. He's asleep with his head on her lap, his exhaustion finally winning out over the licks and tail-wagging.

"I wish he could tell us what happened," CeCe says in a low voice.

"Me, too," I say. "But what matters right now is that we found him."

"We have to tell the police, right? This can't be a coincidence."

"I'll call Detective Milner as soon as we get home. We'll let him decide what to do, okay?"

"How could anyone do something like this? And how do we keep it from happening again?"

"We'll increase our security. Add cameras all the way around the house. I'll work on that tomorrow."

"So we're going to build ourselves a prison?"

"No," I say, shaking my head. "Hopefully, she'll get bored and move on."

"What if she doesn't?"

"Baby, I think we have to address this one step at a time. If we start projecting what-if's, we'll end up living in fear of stepping out of the house."

"It's not right," I say, a slow anger starting to rise inside me. "One person shouldn't have the ability to ruin someone else's life."

"That can only happen if we let it."

"We didn't let her steal Hank Junior today."

"CeCe, we don't know for sure—"

"Holden! This is real. We can't live in denial about it."

"I'm not. We're not. I just think we need to keep it in perspective."

"I don't have any idea what that is. People do crazy things every day. Crazy people do crazy things. It's pretty clear that she's operating on the crazy side."

"Someone like this wants to intimidate, CeCe. Let's not let her do that."

"I am intimidated! What if she does something to you next?"

"I'm not going to let that happen, okay?"

But she doesn't answer me. She wraps her arms around Hank Junior. And we don't say anything else the rest of the way home.

♪

CeCe

I CAN'T SLEEP.

The clock beside our bed says 2:15 AM when I finally get up and go downstairs. Hank Junior hops off the bed and follows me to the kitchen. He hasn't let me out of his sight since we got home.

I pull a bottle of water from the refrigerator and get him a doggy cookie out of the jar on the counter.

I know I shouldn't, but the thought is what's kept me awake for the last few hours, so I give into it.

I sit down in front of the laptop in our office, bringing up the Google search bar and typing in "stalker."

The first thing that comes up is a TV series with that title. The next is a Wikipedia definition. I scroll down until I reach a link to "Stalking Information" from the National Center for Victims of Crime. It says this:

What is stalking?

"a course of conduct directed at a specific person that would cause a reasonable person to feel fear."

Some things stalkers do:

Follow you. Show up wherever you are. Drive by or hang out at your home. Threaten to hurt you, your family, friends or pets.

I refine my search with: stalkers celebrities.

The first result is Craziest Celebrity Stalkers.

Britney Spears. Stalked by Japanese fan claiming to be in love with her. Appeared at her homes, her parents' homes, trying to get in whenever he could.

Beyonce. Fan convinced she was an imposter and that the real Beyonce was dead.

Miley Cyrus. Stalker claimed to be married to her; caught trying to get into her home with a pair of scissors.

John Rich of Big and Rich. Country music star stalked by Nashville attorney for years.

I type in another search phrase. Female stalkers.

I click on a page entitled *Female Stalkers and Their Victims* from PubMed.gov. I scan the information.

> "82 female stalkers from the United States, Canada, and Australia. Female stalkers were predominantly single, heterosexual, educated individuals in their mid 30s who had pursued their victims for more than a year. Major mental disorder and personality disorder were suggested, especially borderline personality disorder. They usually threatened violence, and if they did threaten, were more likely to be violent."

I close out the screen, realizing I'm completely freaking myself out.

We don't even know for sure that she had anything to do with Hank's disappearance. Holden wants to assume that it wasn't her, and I have to admit I'd almost rather find out that it was some random incident not likely to ever happen again.

I reach down to rub Hank's head, newly grateful that he is here, that he is safe.

I know I should go to bed and try not to think about this anymore, but I open Facebook and check the posts. I scroll through, and thankfully, they are all the normal kind.

But then a message pops up at the bottom of the screen.

Is that you online, Holden?

I read the name. Charlotte Gearly.

I force myself to think for a moment, but then impulsively reply.

Yes.
I can't believe my luck.
I think we need to talk.
Can we meet?
This doesn't require meeting.
What is it, then?

This has gotten out of hand.

What do you mean?

Did you steal our dog and take him somewhere?

Seriously?

Yes, seriously.

I like dogs, Holden.

That's not what I asked you.

I wouldn't hurt your dog or any dog.

Someone tried to.

Why would you think it was me?

Why wouldn't I?

You think because I have a crush on you, I would do something like that?

I don't know what to think.

I would never do anything to cause you pain. Just the opposite, in fact.

You need to stop contacting me. No more messages, no more visits. Do you understand?

This isn't Holden, is it?

I start to lie, but fury prompts me to be truthful.

No, it isn't. It's his wife. And I'm telling you to stay away from him.

Aww, that's so sweet, CeCe. You trying to pull the wool over my eyes. Too bad it didn't work, huh?

You are going to get arrested if you keep doing this.

Doing what? Acknowledging a crush on Holden? What would they charge me with? Intent to seduce?

I clench my fists together, feeling my face go red with anger. I delete the messages and close out the page, slamming the lid to the laptop closed.

"What are you doing up, babe?"

I swing around in the chair to find Holden standing in the doorway, shirtless and barefoot, his jeans unbuttoned at the top.

"I—I couldn't sleep," I say. "Just puttering around on the computer."

"Are you okay?" he asks, his voice raspy.

I force myself to take a calming breath, letting my gaze sweep over him. "I just feel like I need to burn some energy," I say.

"Really?" he asks, his eyes widening.

"Yeah. Are you up for assisting?"

He looks at me for a long moment, saying, "It would be ungentlemanly of me to refuse."

"It would."

"Hank, why don't you go check on Patsy?"

Hank gets up from the floor by my chair and trots out the door. Holden closes it behind him. "Now, what were you saying about excess energy?"

I walk over to the window and close the curtain, flicking off the lamp by the sofa. "Maybe you could think of some way to wear me out?"

He smiles and shakes his head a little. "Am I still asleep, and is this a dream?"

"I don't think so. I feel pretty awake."

"Come here," he says.

I walk across the room, slowly, lifting my nightgown and pulling it over my head before dropping it to the floor.

Holden's heated gaze sweeps my face, then falls lower until he has taken in my entire body.

"Do you have any idea what you do to me?" he asks, wrapping his hand around the back of my neck and pulling my mouth to his. He stops just short of kissing me.

He starts with my lower lip, nipping it lightly with his teeth.

"Holden," I say, reaching up to pull his mouth to mine.

But he doesn't let me yet. He presses his lips to the side of my neck, working his way to the center of my throat and then back along the line of my jaw, until his mouth hovers above mine. "What?" he finally asks.

"Kiss me," I say.

And he does, deeply, with none of the tentative play of a few moments before.

I slide my arms up his back, pressing myself as close to him as it is possible to be, arching my neck to drink in the full taste of him. He runs his hand along my spine, and then lifts me up. I wrap my legs around his waist, and he makes a low sound of pleasure-pain.

He carries me to the sofa this way, lowering me onto the cool leather. He follows me down. And as always, I'm amazed by how we fit together, as if we are two pieces of a puzzle destined to find each other, incomplete until we do.

Here, in the darkened room, he makes love to me, his every touch, every kiss, every word leaving me satiated with the knowledge that I am so very lucky to know this kind of love.

Later, much later, when I am curled up tight with my back to his chest, I think about Charlotte and wonder just how far she will go to have him. How far I will have to go to stop her.

♪

Charlotte

I THINK ABOUT the randomness of life on a regular basis.

It's in the front of my mind this morning, while I walk to the market just down from our apartment building to buy breakfast for my dad.

What facet of fate determined that I would end up doing what I do every day, no man in my life except for a father dependent on me to bring him his next artery-clogging meal?

Who got to decide this would be my daily existence, while someone like CeCe MacKenzie Ashford gets to wake up next to Holden?

She's probably a nice girl. If he fell for her, I'm guessing she is. But is it right that I spend my youth, the years when men might actually be interested in me doing what I'm doing?

It's not that I blame her. She just happens to be the roadblock to me making a different life for myself. It's not as if she hasn't had him at all. And I'm sure she'll attract another great guy once they're divorced, because that's what happens for girls like her. They seem to have this natural-born ability to reel in the good guys, the ones that all of us other girls would die to have.

It's a little laughable that she tried to pretend to be Holden last night. As if I wouldn't catch on eventually. Holden would never have said some of those things. He might not realize it completely yet, but he is attracted to me. I've seen it in his eyes when he looks at me, and that is something to grow from.

We just need the opportunity to spend some time together. Which means I need to find out where he's going to be and what he'll be doing in the near future. I know that once he sees how much I care for him, those same feelings will start to grow inside him.

And so today, I'm not going in to work at all. I'll spend some time watching what they're doing, following him around, and making a plan for how we can spend time together.

Once I'm done with the shopping, I carry the bag of food back to the apartment, letting myself in the door and closing it behind me.

The smell hits me in the face, and I instantly press my hand over my mouth and nose. It isn't the first time this has happened, but there are some lines I will not give on. This is one of them.

Holding my breath, I set the bag of food beside my father's chair. He doesn't look at me. He just stares straight ahead at the television screen. I want to scream at him. Make him feel more terrible than I am sure he already feels.

But I don't. Because what is the point?

"I'll call the nurse from the county and see if she can come early today."

And with that, I leave the apartment, wishing I never had to come back again.

♪

Holden

I DRIVE DOWNTOWN to see Detective Milner at ten o'clock.

CeCe is at the house, waiting to meet with the caterer about her mom's party. I decided not to tell her about the appointment with the detective because I'm trying to downplay the whole thing, and admitting that I'm meeting with him will do the opposite.

When I get there, the detective leads me through the main room of the police station. A uniformed female officer walks up and asks for my autograph. I stop to sign the cover of her iPhone case. She smiles and thanks me with the kind of sincerity I still find awkward but am, nevertheless, grateful for. Three other women walk over and hold out some things for me to sign.

Detective Milner says, "All right, ladies, I need to borrow him for a few minutes," before directing me to his office. He closes the door behind us. "Sorry about that."

"It's nice," I say. "I don't mind."

He offers me a chair and then takes the one on the other side of the desk. "I know you didn't want to go into it over the phone, so tell me what happened."

"I believe Charlotte Gearly stole our dog, Hank, from our backyard and dropped him a couple hours away."

"Did you find him?" the detective asks, showing immediate concern.

"We did. His collar had a GPS tracking device on it. We were able to locate the spot where his collar was thrown in the weeds. After a while, we found him nearby."

"Why do you think she did it?"

"Because of everything else that is happening. I believe she might have done this as retaliation against CeCe."

"Because?"

"Because she sees her as a roadblock to me. Damn, that sounds crazy."

"But you think it's true?"

"I do."

"Are you worried about your wife's safety?"

"Of course, I am. I can put up with her saying and doing things that aren't appropriate. But I won't put up with her threatening my wife."

"The first thing I have to advise you of again, Holden, is that you need to let the police handle this. Responding out of anger is just going to land you in jail instead of her."

"So you're saying we have to put up with this until she does something the police can't ignore?"

"Until she does something that is illegal. Do you have any proof that she took your dog?"

"No," I say. "Just a gut feeling."

"I can't arrest her on that."

"Do you have any idea how frustrating this is? To feel that someone is a threat to someone you love and not be able to do anything about it?"

"I think I can imagine, yes."

"I don't want CeCe to know how concerned I am, because I don't want her walking around in fear. At the same time, we have to be realistic about the fact that this woman feels like a threat."

"I'd like for you to have cameras installed that will cover each angle of the outside of your home. If we can get footage of her at your house, that will give us something concrete to go on."

"I'm already working on that. They're supposed to be installed tomorrow."

"Good. I'm actually surprised you don't already have that kind of security. Most folks at your level of success do it proactively."

"Maybe I've been naive then."

He leans back in his chair, his voice concerned when he says, "It's not that. It's actually kind of refreshing to meet someone who doesn't see himself as big as he is. But I've gotta tell you, there are some crazy people in this world. Of course, you already know that."

I nod once.

"We run into them every day," he goes on. "And with the level of exposure you and your wife have in the public eye, you really can't be too careful. There's a country music star here in town who's been dealing with a stalker for years. This stalker has broken into his house while he was on vacation, lived there until he got back just so they could know what it was like to be him. That's some crazy stuff."

I shake my head, disbelieving. "Did the person go to jail?"

"Yeah, but as soon as he got out, he was right back at it again. Keeps his distance for a while, using social media and such to leave messages, but eventually, he can't help himself and crosses a line and ends up back in jail."

"And there's nothing that can be done to stop him?"

"It's kind of a cat-and-mouse thing," he says.

"I would leave the business altogether before I would live like that."

"To be honest, I think I would too. But as I'm sure you know, there's a lot to lose."

I stand, one hand on the back of my chair. "Detective Milner, none of what I have would mean anything to me if I didn't have my wife to share it with. She is who I care about here. Her safety. I will do whatever I have to do to protect her."

"And I will do whatever I can within the limits of the law to help you. I hope it will be enough."

The words are more than a little unsettling. I leave his office, walking out of the station without meeting eyes with anyone as I go. Worry and fear are a boulder on my chest. I had hoped to leave here feeling reassured about some course of action that we could take.

I don't feel reassured at all.

♪

Charlotte

HOLDEN'S LAND ROVER isn't in the driveway, but CeCe's car is.

There's also a minivan with *Smash Hit Catering* written on the side. They must be planning an event. I wonder what kind.

I Google the catering business and surprise, surprise, it's *the* "party to the stars" catering establishment in Nashville.

I glance at the menu options and realize I've never heard of most of the dishes they prepare for the hoity-toity. When money is no option, I guess you can afford the exotic.

I wonder when the party will be. And if I could possibly get an invitation.

After last night's messaging with CeCe, I think not.

But then that isn't the only way to gain entrance. What if I could get a job with the caterer?

I hate my current job, and I'm about to get fired anyway for the days I've been missing and not calling in.

But I have no experience in catering or the food industry. What's the likelihood of me getting hired?

Not that great.

But then who says my experience has to be real? People make up resumes all the time. And I'm nothing if not creative.

The front door opens, and a woman with long black hair walks out. She's smiling and saying something over her shoulder. CeCe steps out behind her then, and I pull away from the curb before she sees me.

Next stop: the library.

♪

CeCe

I WAVE AS Millie Turner backs out of the driveway and pulls out into the street. She's a really nice lady, willing to take on our party for Mama, even though it's less than a week away.

I'm supposed to meet Holden and Thomas at a studio on Music Row in half an hour. I grab my purse, call for Hank and Patsy and help them in the car, Hank in the front seat of the 911 and Patsy in the mini backseat.

I open the sunroof and Hank stands to stick his nose out, breathing in the fresh air and looking as if he's trying to decide what some of the scents are.

I reach across and rub his head, glad to have the dogs with me. I'm not comfortable leaving them at home now, even inside the house.

When I arrive at the studio, Thomas is just pulling in. He gets out of his truck and walks over to my side of the car. I get out and give him a hug.

"You brought the crew today, huh?"

"Hank is wondering if he can do background vocals," I say.

"He's got the baritone for it," Thomas says, smiling.

I hand him a leash, and he gets Patsy out of the back while I walk around and get Hank from the other side.

"How are you?" Thomas asks, as we walk toward the stone building.

"Honestly?"

He raises an eyebrow, and we stop beside a patch of grass where Hank and Patsy do their business.

"Rattled, I guess. Have you talked to Holden?"

"Just for a minute this morning," he says.

"Someone took Hank out of our backyard yesterday. We found him two hours away by using the tracking device on his collar."

"What?" he asks, shocked.

"He and Patsy were in the fenced yard, and then Hank was just gone."

"Who do you think—"

"I think it was Charlotte Gearly, the woman who's hot after Holden."

"Why would she do that?"

"I don't know. Because she's crazy."

"Damn," Thomas says. "Did y'all call the police?"

"Holden did. They're saying they can't arrest her, unless we have evidence that she took him."

"If only he could talk," Thomas says, reaching down to rub Hank's head.

"It was awful," I say, tears filling my eyes. "Thinking we weren't going to be able to find him."

He pulls me to him then, kissing the top of my head. "What can I do, honey?"

I shake my head, wiping a hand across my face. "It's like our hands are tied. I didn't tell Holden this, but she messaged him last night when I was on Facebook. She is definitely not playing with a full deck."

"Why didn't you tell him?"

"Because he's already worried sick."

"You can't close him out, CeCe. You need his protection."

"I'm not. But this thing last night, I could handle. It's like she's fixated on him, and I'm in the way."

"You know people like that do some insane crap."

"She looks so normal. Just a pretty girl who could probably get most any guy she wants."

"Just not *the* guy she wants."

"Well, no," I say. "I'm not giving her mine."

"Now that's the girl I picked up on I-40 when her car caught on fire."

I smile and punch his arm. "Shades of me," I say.

"I wouldn't want to try to take him away from you."

'There have been times when I wondered," I say, teasing.

"All right now," he says, and gooses me through the door.

♪

Holden

SOMETIMES, I WISH it could just go back to being about making music for the love of making music.

We're in the studio playing through "R U Serious" for the fifth or sixth time, CeCe and Thomas smoothing the edges of the verses and then the chorus, the producer offering some advice on the bridge.

This is the part of what we do that I truly love. Creating a song, bringing it to life, refining it until we feel as if it's something we can be proud of. This is the part of what we do that I feel is in my control. And although I don't think I could say it to CeCe and Thomas now, I wonder if life out of the spotlight would be a better choice. Writing and producing for someone else, maybe.

That's easier said than done. We've built a career that I've been proud of, and I know the same is true for CeCe and Thomas.

I guess it's just that things don't seem so simple anymore. Our love for what we do — writing, recording, performing — feels as if it's taken a backseat to everything else that's involved.

I listen now as CeCe and Thomas nail the chorus this time. And I see the satisfaction on their faces. I realize, too, that there are a lot of people who will get happiness from hearing them sing it. Aren't those the people I should be focusing on? Instead of the one person who is intent on stealing the joy we find in what we do?

I don't want to let her do that. Which means I'm going to have to trust that we'll find our way through this. That eventually, she will get tired of the game and go away.

♪

Charlotte

I HAVE TO wonder what people did before the Internet.

Answers to pretty much any question you can think of to ask are literally at your fingertips.

Name of a five-star restaurant in Seattle? Check. Owner? Check. Head chef? Check.

Catering company in San Francisco? Check. Contact information? Check.

I pull the relevant pieces of information from the websites, using each like bricks to a foundation until I have built myself an admirable resume. I type it up on the library computer, using one of their handy resume templates, so that the final outcome is pretty darn impressive.

I print out five copies, pay the librarian at the front desk my $1.25, and stick them in an envelope so they won't get wrinkled.

Next, I drive to a nearby drugstore, not sure I'm going to go through with it until I'm actually standing in the aisle of hair-care products. I find a brand of blonde that is as close to matching hers as it can be and then take it to the front register to pay for it.

Two things I hope to accomplish here. One, if CeCe is Holden's type, then I can be that. He likes what he likes. Nothing wrong with that. And anyway, I've always wondered what I would look like with blonde hair. And two, if I can get a job catering their upcoming event, I don't want them to recognize me.

That is the only way the rest of my plan stands a hope of working.

♪

Holden

OVER THE NEXT few days, I find myself waiting for Charlotte to appear out of nowhere, show up on our Facebook page or call our house.

But it turns out that none of those things happen. The camera installation is completed within a day, and although it feels weird to be able to see every angle of our house by checking the monitor in the office, it is also reassuring.

On Wednesday night, Thomas and I work on a song at his place until just after nine. When I get home, I call for CeCe, but there's no answer. Her car is in the driveway, so I know that she's here. And all the lights are on.

"CeCe?"

Still no answer.

The dogs aren't around either. My heart starts to pound, and, after checking the kitchen, I take the stairs two at a time to our room. "CeCe?"

"In here," she calls out from behind the closed bathroom door.

I knock, closing my eyes and exhaling in relief. "All right if I come in?"

"Sure," she says. "The door isn't locked."

I step in and close the door behind me. She's in the tub, bubbles up to her chin, her face breaking into a smile at the sight of me. Hank Junior and Patsy are on the rug next to the whirlpool tub, both of them asleep.

"Hey," she says.

"Hey."

"Are you okay?"

"I just got a little worried when you didn't answer right away."

"I'm sorry. I didn't hear you."

"I know. Ordinarily, I wouldn't think anything, but—"

"I'm jumpy too."

"We need to stop."

"I'm trying."

"Me too."

"There's room in here for two," she says.

"Yeah?"

"Yeah," she says, patting down the bubbles so that her bare shoulders are now visible.

I start to unbutton my shirt. "That's the best invitation I've had all day."

"And the only one of its kind, I hope," she says.

I laugh and slide into the tub behind her.

♪

CeCe

MAMA AND AUNT VERA arrive at the airport on Thursday afternoon. I pick them up out front at Mama's insistence. They walk through the sliding doors at the main terminal entrance, Mama pulling her sedate, single black piece of luggage, Vera rolling a fat pink suitcase that could double as a smart car.

I get out and walk around to greet them, opening my arms to give them both a hug. "I'm so happy you're here," I say.

Mama kisses me on one cheek, Vera kisses me on the other.

"It's so good to see our little star," Vera says.

"Aunt Vera—" I start, helping them put the luggage in the back of Holden's Land Rover.

"Well, now it's true, CeCe. Don't be denying it and getting all humble on us."

"Vera, CeCe just wants to be her regular self with us," Mama says. "Don't fluster her."

"Fluster her? Well, for goodness sakes," Aunt Vera says, climbing in the backseat. "I would say she's earned the accolades. They've had four number one songs on the Billboard chart."

I smile and shake my head, pulling away from the curb and merging with the cars leaving the airport. "Now y'all stop fussing, and let's talk about your party, Mama."

"CeCe," she says, "I sure hope you didn't go to an awful lot of trouble."

"What trouble?" Vera protests. "Your only daughter has planned you a birthday celebration. She doesn't consider that trouble, do you, CeCe?"

"Aunt Vera, you know I long ago vowed not to get in between you and Mama when you aren't seeing eye to eye. I'm not starting today."

Aunt Vera sniffs. "Fair enough. But tell us about the guest list. Who all's invited? Blake and Miranda? Tim and Faith?"

"Well, if that's not the silliest thing I've ever heard, Vera," Mama says. "Why on earth would they want to come to my birthday party? They don't even know me."

"They know CeCe and Holden. It seems logical to me. Are they invited, CeCe?" Aunt Vera asks again.

"I think we'll let the guest list be a surprise," I say, shaking my head.

"Any eligible country music hunks?" she asks. "Approximately my age?"

"Vera," Mama says, "this is not going to be a repeat of Las Vegas. It was a downright disgrace the way you flirted with those waiters serving the drinks."

"Did you happen to notice I didn't pay for any of mine?" she asks on a huffy note.

"And you're proud of that?" Mama asks.

"As a matter of fact, I am. There's pointless flirting. And there's productive flirting. Mine was of the productive variety."

"And there's a woman acting her age, and then there's not," Mama says pointedly.

"You mean like a woman who throws away a chance at happiness with a dreamboat like Case Phillips?"

Mama folds her arms across her chest and stares out the window, refusing to take the bait.

By now, I feel compelled to change the subject. "Holden has a stalker."

"What?" Mama and Aunt Vera say in unison, alarm lacing their voices.

"Or maybe we both do. I don't know."

"What do you mean, CeCe?" Mama asks.

I tell her then, everything that's happened to date. Mama and Vera sit quietly while I do, and I can already feel Mama's worry building like a summer storm. When I'm finished, she reaches across and puts her hand on my arm.

"Why don't y'all leave this business, CeCe? All of you have already been through a nightmare because of a crazy person's hatred. I can't stand the thought that you might be in danger again."

"Don't worry, Mama. Please. We're taking extra precautions. The police are involved to what extent they can be. I think she'll lose interest at some point."

In the rear view mirror, I see Aunt Vera shake her head. "I don't know, CeCe. People who fixate on someone live in their own reality. I watched this documentary on that actress Rebecca, what was her name?"

"Schaeffer, I think," Mama says. She played in that sitcom, *My Sister Sam.*"

"That's right," Aunt Vera says. "This man had been stalking her for something like three years. He walked right up to her apartment door and shot and killed her."

"I shouldn't have told you," I say.

"How could you not?" Mama asks, her voice rising a little.

"It will just make you worry all the time."

"And shouldn't I?" she says.

"Worry doesn't do any good," Aunt Vera says. "But you do have to be smart about these things, honey. You just don't know what another person is thinking."

"We're being careful. We've had extra cameras installed in and around our house."

"It's like you're living in a prison," Mama says. "Are you sure it's worth that?"

"It's probably sounding worse than it is," I say. "And anyway, this weekend is not about that. It's about celebrating your birthday. So let's talk about that."

"Yes," Aunt Vera says. "Back to the guest list."

♪

Holden

I TURN CECE'S 911 into the driveway leading to Case Phillips's house. I called an hour or so ago to make sure that he would be home and that it was okay to drop by.

He'd sounded surprised to hear from me, and I realize how long it's been since we've seen each other.

I park at the front of the house, get out, and knock on the door. He answers it himself, smiling at me and sticking out his hand.

"Hey, Case," I say. "I hope I'm not catching you in the middle of something."

"Nope," he says. "Come on in, Holden. I finished up a writing session with Rivers this morning, so I'm goofing off the rest of the day."

"Thanks for letting me drop by," I say.

"You know you're welcome anytime," he says, waving me down the hall that leads to his studio at the back of the house. Memories of our early days in Nashville drift up. In a way, that seems like an entire lifetime ago. Pictures of Beck line the walls, and it hits me with fresh remorse what a tragedy it is that his life ended as it did.

"Come on in," Case says, closing the door of the studio behind us.

"How are you, Case?" I ask.

His gaze meets mine, and it's clear that my question is not a casual one. "I have days here and there," he says.

"I'm sorry," I say.

"I know. And thank you. Life just doesn't prepare us for losing those we love the most. There's a hole there that nothing can ever fill."

I want to say something that might in some way be helpful, but I know that there is nothing. "You know if there's anything we can ever do, you only have to ask."

"I do know that. And I can't tell you how much I appreciate it. Everything going all right with you guys? Heard your new single has hit written all over it."

"We'll see," I say. "This independent route is a different ball game."

"If I were your age, that's what I'd be doing. I'm too old to reinvent the wheel though."

"Those women trying to tear your clothes off at concerts don't seem to think you're too old for anything."

Case smiles and shakes his head. "You here about the invitation to Mira's party?" he asks, getting to the point.

"Since we hadn't heard back from you, CeCe asked me if I would talk to you," I say.

"Sorry about that," he says. "I've been dragging my feet on the RSVP, because I really think it's best if I don't come."

"Because you and Mrs. MacKenzie broke up?"

"She wouldn't want me there."

"CeCe seems to think differently."

"The last time we talked, well, it wasn't good."

"Mind if I ask what happened?"

Case sighs. "I guess our lives were just too different."

"It seemed like you loved each other."

"I know I loved her."

"But she didn't think she could keep your interest?"

"Something like that. I guess my reputation preceded me."

"Do you still care about her?"

Case looks off out the window for a moment and then meets my gaze. "I do."

"They why don't you come, Case? You probably know this a lot better than I do, but sometimes I think our women need us to convince them."

He shakes his head a little. "You're speaking from experience, I take it?"

"Yeah," I say, conceding. "I am."

♪

CeCe

WE'RE IN THE KITCHEN having a glass of wine when Holden gets home.

He walks right over to Mama and scoops her up off her chair in a bear hug that has her giggling like a teenager. When he puts her back down, he does the same to Aunt Vera, and I have to think if he could bottle this charm he has with the female sex, we wouldn't need to make another record.

"I don't know if this house can handle so much beauty all at once."

"Now, Holden Ashford," Aunt Vera says, "you know you shouldn't go getting a girl's hopes up."

"Yes, ma'am," he says, leaning down to give her a kiss on the cheek.

It takes a lot to make Aunt Vera swoon, but she's pretty much there.

Holden comes over and gives me a kiss on the mouth. "You ready for me to fire up the grill?"

"I've got all the vegetables cut up. They're in the fridge. Thomas and Lila and Lexie will be here around six."

"I'd better get started then," he says.

"Glass of wine?" I ask.

"Yeah," he says. "Any red open?"

"I'll open one. I'd like some too."

Mama stands and takes Aunt Vera's hand, pulling her up from her chair. "We need to go powder our noses before your company gets here."

"But I just powdered—" Aunt Vera begins.

"You're shiny," Mama says, as they leave the kitchen.

"Those two," I say, shaking my head.

Holden hooks an arm around my waist and pulls me up against him, kissing me softly.

"What's that for?" I ask, feeling the tenderness in his kiss.

"I'm just grateful," he says. "That I have you. That we have each other."

"You went to see Case?"

101

"Yeah. He seems so lonely. That big house and all those accolades on the walls of his studio. But he's alone."

"I know. What did he say about the party?"

"That he didn't think your mama would want him here."

"I think she doesn't want to admit to herself that she's in love with him."

"I'm not sure we'll come out all that good getting involved in this."

"You're probably right. I just thought if he came, they might have a chance to talk and—"

"I'm not sure he's going to."

"I guess I'll have to be content to leave it at that," I say.

"Which does not suit you at all," he says.

"Now, now. Are you implying that I like to have my way?"

"Me?"

"It is possible that I like to have my way with you."

"And if your mama and your aunt weren't in this house right now, I'd call you on that one."

I laugh and push him away. "We could make out in the pantry."

"Until Vera comes in looking for those cookies she likes."

"It takes a lot to make Aunt Vera blush."

Holden backs away from me, his hands in the air. "If I don't get outside to the grill, you and I both are definitely going to end up in the pantry."

Hank Junior gets up from his spot beside my chair, trots to the back door and barks once.

"See," I say. "He's trying to keep you out of trouble."

"Coming, Hank," he says. "We'll continue this later tonight. Upstairs. Date?"

"Date," I say and smile.

♪

Charlotte

I'M HOLDING MY breath as Millie Turner reads over my resume. I'm sitting across from her in my best classic black dress, the neckline modest, the cut flattering but not too fitting. I'm wearing low-heel, sensible shoes that I hope help portray me as a hard-working, not overly interested in meeting celebrities girl.

"I'm so glad you ended up having time to meet with me, Ms. Turner," I say. "It's obvious you're incredibly busy."

"Well, having a much relied-on employee quit right before an important event kind of throws things in a tailspin."

I think about that much relied-on employee and the call I'd had with her earlier today. I pretended to be the owner of Smash Hit Catering's biggest competitor, Cadence Catering, offering her a job, at twenty-five percent above what she is currently making, to start on Monday. I also let her know that rumor had it that Ms. Turner was no longer satisfied with her work and had been scouting some of Cadence's employees to take her place. By the time I actually offered her the job, she could hardly wait to start.

Not to be unkind now, but Ms. Turner looks as if she's been in a tailspin most of the day. Her hair, which apparently started out in a neat bun, has escaped its clasp, sticking out in unruly wisps that she swipes at every minute or so. I suppose I shouldn't take pleasure in other people's misery, but there is some actual enjoyment to be had in manipulation. It's sort of like moving pieces on a chessboard, with insider knowledge.

"You worked in Seattle?" Ms. Turner asks me now.

"Yes, ma'am."

"Were you born there?"

"No, here in Nashville. I just wanted to see the country and decided to live in some different places."

"And San Francisco."

"Yes."

"What was your main responsibility at each of these establishments?"

"Helping do prep work before catering events and serving during

103

the event. I can also bartend." At least that piece is true, I think, remembering that someone once said the best lies are sprinkled with truth.

"Charlotte, rest assured I will follow up on your resume, checking your references and such. But based on what I see here, I'm going to go ahead and hire you. Can you start tomorrow?"

"Of course," I say. "When is your next event?"

"Saturday evening," she says. "A party for the Ashfords. CeCe and Holden."

"Of Barefoot Outlook?" I ask.

"Yes," she says, and I can feel her watching me to see if I'm too giddy about the idea, likely to go starstruck on spotting them or their guests.

I keep my expression perfectly neutral. "How exciting," I say.

♪

CeCe

WE EAT OUTSIDE on the terrace. Holden and Thomas handle the grill and are responsible for the food turning out great.

They talk about music, of course, NASCAR racing, and this book Thomas has been reading about juicing. He's determined to get Holden to try it.

Lila, Mama, Aunt Vera and I talk about girl stuff. Mama and Aunt Vera are completely smitten with Lexie. She draws them each a picture, and I think if they could steal her and sneak her back home with them, there's no question that they would.

Lila and I move our chairs closer together so we can chat. I'm thrilled to hear that she's feeling really good about the song she is writing.

"It's so nice to hear that enthusiasm in your voice," I say.

"Thank you, CeCe. I don't know. I just have a very different outlook on things these days. I want to wring every drop of joy I can possibly get out of my life. You know, the leave no stone unturned kind of thing."

"It shouldn't take a life quake to make us all realize that's what we need to be doing."

"Life quake," she says. "That's pretty much it. And sad to say, I think it does take that for most of us."

"Thomas has told you about the woman—"

"Stalker?" she says.

"Yeah. It's kind of shaken me up."

"Understandably," Lila says. "Is it still going on?"

"I hope not. The last few days there's been no sign of her."

"It's not right that someone can deliberately disrupt your life like that."

"I didn't tell Holden this, but she messaged while I was on Facebook the other night. At first she thought she was talking with him, but once she figured out it wasn't him, she really creeped me out."

"What did she say?"

"It's like she really believed that Holden and I will get tired of each other, and she'll be there waiting for him."

"Wow."

"I know. It's more than disturbing to think you're occupying another person's thoughts like that."

"CeCe, you need to be careful. You can't predict what someone like that will do."

"I will be. And Holden has gone Rambo on me. We have all these cameras now. I don't think there's a spot in the house that's not covered. I don't like living like that."

"With all the good that comes with being successful in this business, there's some not so good too," Lila says.

Thomas walks up, leans over and kisses the top of Lila's head. "What are you two plotting?"

"A way to remove the bad people from the world. Can't we just put them all on an island or something? They can be mean to one another and leave the rest of us alone."

"I like it," Thomas says. "*Lord of the Flies* business."

"Sounds like a perfect idea to me," I say.

"What?" Holden asks, walking over and massaging my shoulders.

"Lila wants to put all bad people on an island," Thomas says.

"The way things are going, it'll have to be an awfully big island," Holden says.

"Let's turn this conversation to dessert," I say, standing, "before we get too depressed to eat it."

♪

Holden

WE SPEND MOST OF SATURDAY getting the house ready for the party. It's late afternoon by the time CeCe and I head upstairs to change. I crash on the bed, deciding to take a quick nap while she's in the shower.

I'm halfway asleep when I realize the shower hasn't started. I wait a few minutes more, then get up and knock on the door. "Hey, babe, are you all right?"

"Yes," she says, unconvincing.

"Can I come in?"

"It's not locked."

I turn the knob and stick my head in. She's sitting on the side of the tub, elbows on her knees, face in her hands.

"What's wrong?" I ask, suddenly concerned.

"Maybe nothing. I'm not sure."

"Are you okay?" I walk over and sit down beside her.

She raises her left hand. She's holding a pregnancy test and there's a + sign in the small window.

"Are you telling me that we're—"

"Pregnant," she finishes, her expression uncertain.

I drop to my knees on the floor in front of her. "When did you start to suspect?"

"I'm a few days late. But I really didn't think this would come up positive."

I set the test on the edge of the tub, take her hands in mine. "We're going to have a baby."

She bites her lower lip. "Are you okay with that?"

"Okay? I'm like — CeCe — a baby."

She smiles, shaking her head a little. "I know. Us. A mama and daddy."

"Come here," I say, sliding my arms around her and kissing her softly on the mouth. "You are going to be the most beautiful pregnant woman ever."

"You might be a tad bit biased," she says.

I raise her shirt and kiss her very flat belly. "Hi, baby," I say. "Tonight when we go to bed, I'm going to sing to you. And every night between now and the time you join us in this world."

CeCe rubs her hand across my hair, and when I lean back to look at her, she has tears in her eyes. "My gosh, I love you," she says.

"My gosh, I love you."

♪

Charlotte

I TURN OFF the blow dryer and stare at myself in the mirror.

I should have gone blonde long ago. I even love my eyebrows lightened like this.

I turn and take in the length of my smooth hair. It's a shame to put it up when it looks this good, but the Smash Hit Catering Employee Expectation Handbook that Ms. Turner gave me to read over insists that everyone has to wear their hair up when preparing food or working in a service position.

That's me tonight. Working in a service position.

My stomach drops a little at the thought of actually being inside Holden's house. I keep thinking something will happen to make all of this fall through. Like Ms. Turner getting around to calling my references in Seattle. So far though, she hasn't, and with the party a few hours away, I can't imagine she's going to find time to do so. Trust is a beautiful thing.

I pull my hair back in a classic bun, apply my makeup, not too much, but just enough. I add a pink lipstick and then slip into the black dress I'm to wear to the party. I turn to look at myself in the full-length mirror hanging on the back of the bathroom door.

I'll be the little brown wren in comparison to all the other women at the party, but that's okay. I don't plan to stay one forever. And it's uncanny that I actually look a little like CeCe with my hair this color.

I walk through my bedroom and out into the living room, hoping Dad will be asleep, saving me the explanation of the new hair, but of course, he isn't.

"Wow," he says. "That's quite a change."

"I needed one," I say, short. I pull a large box of pizza from the refrigerator, consider heating it up as I usually do, then decide against it. I need to go, and it won't matter to him whether it's hot or cold.

I carry it over to the table beside his chair and set it down. "Do you have something to drink?" I ask.

He points at the Bubba container on the coffee table in front of him. "Still have some Coke in there. Why are you dressed like that?"

"I have a new job," I say.

"Doing what?" he asks, trying to sound interested, when I'm sure he would much rather focus on the pizza.

"Working for a caterer," I say.

"Well, that's great. Wonder if they'll send you home with leftovers."

I try not to roll my eyes, but merely turn around, grab my purse and walk out.

♪

CeCe

I CAN'T HELP it. I have to tell Mama. And of course, Aunt Vera as well.

Mama presses a hand to her mouth, and says, "Oh, CeCe. That's just . . . so very wonderful."

She steps forward to pull me into her arms, hugging me tight. Aunt Vera reaches out to rub a hand across my hair.

"I'm so happy for you, sweet girl," she says.

We're in Mama's room, and I close the door to give us some privacy since some of the catering staff has started to arrive.

"Well, I guess I'm like three minutes pregnant," I say, "but the test was positive."

Mama laughs and hugs me again. "I'm going to be a grandma. Oh, my goodness, that is just the best birthday present I've ever gotten."

I smile. "I hadn't thought of that," I say.

"We should just cancel the party," she says. "This is all the celebration I need."

"Oh, no you don't," Aunt Vera says. "You don't get to use CeCe's good news as an excuse to get out of this party."

"It's going to be fun," I say. "Y'all finish getting dressed and I'll see you downstairs, okay?"

"All right, honey," Mama says. "You be careful and don't get too tired or overdo."

"I won't, Mama," I say, pressing my hand to my stomach, and meaning what I just said. Already, I am overcome with the desire to protect the sweet little life growing there. A life Holden and I made together out of love.

♪

Holden

CECE AND I stand at the front door, greeting guests as they come in. The turnout is amazing, considering how quickly we put the party together. The house is packed within thirty minutes.

When there's a lull in the traffic, I lean in and whisper in CeCe's ear. "You look good enough to eat in that dress, but all I want to do is take it off you."

She smiles at me, and says, "You are aware of my condition, aren't you, sir?"

I groan a little. "Are you aware of mine?"

She giggles at this and then blanks her expression just as Case walks in the door.

"Oh, you came," she says, launching herself at him for a hug.

"I hope it's all right," he says, kissing her cheek.

"It's more than all right," CeCe tells him.

"Good heavens, you look gorgeous tonight," he says. "I can see you're keeping her happy, Holden."

"I do my best," I say, smiling.

"Come on," CeCe says, taking his hand. "Let's get you into the mix here."

"I'll find you in a bit," I call after her, and she blows me a kiss.

Hank Junior and Patsy are already making their rounds from guest to guest, scoring big on ham biscuits and sausage balls. I spot Thomas by the fireplace, talking with Lewis, our manager, and make my way over.

"Hey, Holden," Lewis says. "Quite the shindig. The food is incredible."

"Good," I say. "But I have to give CeCe the credit."

I look at Thomas. "Where's Lila?"

"I think she's talking to CeCe's mama. I left them in the kitchen sharing cobbler recipes."

"Actually, I'm glad I've got you two for a moment," Lewis says. "Can we talk a little business?"

"Sure," I say.

Thomas nods.

"I've booked some awesome venues," Lewis says. "We'll start the tour in six weeks. That sound good to y'all?"

I start to immediately say yes, but instantly realize that things have changed. Our life has changed. CeCe is pregnant. And it's not just the two of us to think about anymore. "I'll get with CeCe on it. Thomas, you'll talk with Lila?"

"I think she's got me convinced it's time to do this again."

I nod and say, "Thomas, could I see you alone for a minute?"

"Sure," he says, looking at me with a raised eyebrow.

"Lewis, we'll catch you later, okay?"

"Okay," he says and heads for the bar.

We thread our way through the crowd, finally making it to the office door. I pull him inside.

"What the heck, Holden?" Thomas asks, with a look of surprise. "You know people might talk."

"Shut up," I say. "I have important news."

"What?" he asks, suspicious now.

"We're having a baby."

Thomas leans back. "Whoa. I did not see that one coming. Really?"

"Really."

"Well, all right, man."

"I know."

He throws his arms around me and hugs me hard. "I'm going to be an uncle. Sort of."

"Can you believe it? Me? A daddy?"

"Is that why you hesitated on the tour thing?"

"It just hit me. I'm assuming CeCe will still want to go, but I don't know."

"Have y'all been trying?"

"We haven't *not* been trying."

"Hey, now, we're both gonna be daddys."

"Who would have thought, huh?"

"It's all good, you know. I don't even have words to describe how good it is. Making something as precious as a child with the woman you love beyond reason. It just doesn't get any better. Congratulations, friend."

I lean against the wall of the pantry, folding my arms across my chest. "It's been a hell of a ride so far, hasn't it?"

"You mean since we got to Nashville?"

"Yeah."

"I try not to take a minute of it for granted."

"I don't want to either. You think it's too much to try to hold onto the kind of career we've had and build a family?"

"I guess time will tell," he says.

♪

Charlotte

THE HOUSE IS every bit as incredible as I imagined it. Enormous rooms with ceilings so high I can't imagine what the heating bills must be.

The furnishings look like they came straight out of *Restoration Hardware,* oversize sofas and chairs arranged in groupings, each with their own end tables. The lamps are tall with rustic finishes and throw warm, inviting light across the rooms.

My tiny apartment would fit in the middle of the living room with a ton of space left over. I feel embarrassed by the thought of how I live compared to them. But then I remind myself that it's not my fault, not something I can help. At least until things take a turn for the better.

Starting tonight.

I touch the small vial in the pocket of my dress, making sure it's still there. I need to quit checking, but I'm afraid of losing it and not having it when the time is right.

Mia, one of the waitresses passing around food, comes into the kitchen with an empty tray. "These biscuits are going like hot cakes," she says, and then laughs at what she's just said. "Or like biscuits, I guess," she adds.

"Good to know they like them," I say, removing the Saran Wrap from another platter and handing it to her. "Let me know when you'd like to switch places," she says.

"I'm happy enough in here," I say.

"You don't want to check out the who's who of Nashville? I can't even believe who all's out there."

"Maybe I will," I say. "If you can do something for me."

"What?"

"Ms. Turner wants Mrs. Ashford to try the white wine before we begin passing it. Can you take her a glass?"

"Sure," Mia says. "But if you do it, you could meet her."

"I already have," I say. And then realizing I should sound more enthusiastic, I add, "She's lovely."

117

"Okay. Better hurry though. The biscuits are in high demand."

"Let me just get the wine from the butler's pantry."

I grab a glass and head for the pantry where the bottle of wine has already been opened. I pour it half-full and then take the vial from my pocket, adding the clear liquid.

I think about the cat we had when I was growing up and how our neighbor poisoned him with this same kind of liquid. It was a horrible death and not one I'm happy even delivering to CeCe. But it will do the trick. And in the end, it's the result that I'm after.

♪

CeCe

MAMA AND CASE are doing everything possible to ignore each other. They're on opposite ends of the living room, backs to each other. And yet, I can feel the tension between them.

I finally decide to take matters into my own hands and walk up to Case. "Have you had a chance to say happy birthday to Mama yet?"

He glances down at his boots and then meets my gaze with a reluctant, "No, but I'm going to."

"Come on," I say. "I need to check on her anyway. Make sure she's having a good time."

"CeCe, I'm not sure it's a good idea."

"Why?" I ask. "I thought you two meant a lot to each other at one point."

"So did I," he says. "I'm not the one who broke things off."

"Do you still care about her?"

"I always will," he says, his voice husky with emotion.

"She's scared, Case."

"Of what?"

"Of loving you and losing you."

"She lost me because she didn't want me anymore."

"She pushed you away, because she was scared she wouldn't have what it takes to keep you. And that's a very different thing."

"Did she tell you that?"

"She didn't have to. She's my mama. I doubt anyone knows her better than I do."

I can tell he wants to believe me, but it's clear that he's been hurt. "I don't blame you for not wanting to put yourself on the line again. But I think you two have what it takes to make each other happy. And it's really painful to see you throw it away."

"I'll say happy birthday, CeCe. But if it goes beyond that, it'll have to be because your mama wants it there."

"Fair enough," I say, and take his arm.

♪

Charlotte

I'M PASSING OUT the platter of biscuits, trying to keep my back to CeCe while still sneaking a glance every few seconds.

Mia walks up to her, offers her the glass of wine and explains, I'm sure, that Ms. Turner wanted her to try it.

I offer another guest a ham biscuit, and when I look back, CeCe is shaking her head. She leans in close to Mia and says something. Mia's face breaks into a smile. She nods and puts the glass back on its tray, heading for the kitchen.

Wondering what CeCe said, I step inside a room that looks like an office, dump the remaining biscuits in the trash can and return to the kitchen as well.

Mia glances up and says, "Wow, those went fast. We better load up and get back out there."

"Did she like the wine?" I ask.

Mia looks around and then says in a whisper, "She's pregnant. Can you believe she told me that? I mean, I must be like one of the only people in Nashville who knows. She's not even showing."

I draw in a sharp breath, feeling as if someone has just swung a wrecking ball into my chest. "What?"

"They're having a baby," Mia says, looking at me as if I'm a little dense. "She doesn't want to drink. That's understandable. I was looking for Ms. Turner to ask if I should go ahead with the wine—"

"I'll tell her," I say quickly, taking the tray and glass from her.

"Okay, then, I'll get back to serving." She picks up a full tray of biscuits and heads for the door, turning to add, "You know you kind of look like her."

"Who?"

"CeCe."

"Really?" I ask, trying not to look too impressed.

"Quite a bit, actually."

"Think I could pull a fast one on Holden?" I ask in a low voice.

Mia giggles. "I don't know about that. But maybe if it was dark."

I smile, as if I'm totally kidding.

Once Mia leaves the kitchen, I pour the wine down the sink and drop the glass in the trash can. No point in accidentally killing an innocent person.

I step inside the pantry then and close the door. Frustration and fury melt inside me until my lungs feel clogged with it.

How could this have happened? I had everything planned out. And she's ruined it all.

I drag in several deep breaths, forcing myself to be calm. If I'm not calm, I can't think. If I can't think, I can't come up with a way around this.

One thing I know. Bringing a baby into the picture will change everything. Holden will feel obligated to stay married to her. She'll be the mother of his child.

She cannot have that baby.

She cannot.

♪

CeCe

IT'S ALMOST NINE when we decide it's time to cut Mama's birthday cake.

She and Case have been talking all night. And I can tell by the look on her face that she's glad he's here. Just the thought that they might find a way to get past their differences makes me so happy. It seems a waste for them to be alone when they obviously love each other. At one point, Aunt Vera and I meet eyes. She gives me a conspiratorial thumbs up.

The cake is a three-layer work of art, and two of the catering staff roll it into the living room where everyone has gathered around. Case stands a little to the side while Holden and Thomas and I play and sing "Happy Birthday" to Mama. Everyone joins in, and her eyes are filled with such appreciation that tears fill my eyes.

She leans in and kisses me on the cheek, saying, "I don't know what I did to ever deserve a daughter like you. Thank you, sweetheart. Thank you so much."

I hug her, and everyone claps and cheers. Case steps forward and kisses her on the cheek. Mama blushes and then puts her arm around his neck, holding him close for a long enough time that it's clear something has changed between them. When she pulls back, he takes her hand and doesn't let go.

The wait staff begins passing out plates of cake. Holden pulls me into his office, closing the door behind us. He leans in and kisses me so thoroughly that I lose thought of the fact that we have a house full of guests. I slip my arms around his neck and kiss him back.

"Umm," I say. "To what do I owe the honor?"

"I can't quit thinking about this," he says, placing his hand on my belly. "You've made me so happy, CeCe."

"We're incredibly lucky," I say. "To have each other. Sometimes, I wonder—"

"Don't," he says, touching a finger to my lips. "I don't like questioning it. I just want to be grateful for it."

"I know," I say. "And I am."

"We better get back out there," he says. "How many more hours before I get you all to myself?"

"You know I turn into a pumpkin at midnight."

"Then everyone has to leave before then," he says, kissing me quickly before opening the door. And we go back to the party.

♪

Charlotte

IT'S NOT THAT EASY coming up with a plan on the fly.

Desperation creates mistakes. And that I can't afford to make.

But when I notice CeCe's mom and that hunky Case Phillips slipping out the terrace door to the backyard, I decide I have to act quickly. And Mia — crazy about CeCe Mia — will have to help me.

♪

CeCe

I'M TALKING WITH Thomas and Lila when the nice young woman who had offered me wine earlier walks up and says, "I'm sorry to interrupt, ma'am."

"That's okay. Everything all right?"

"Yes. But apparently your mother needs you upstairs for a moment."

"Really?" I ask. "Is anything wrong?"

"I'm not sure," she says. "I believe she's in her bedroom."

"Okay, thank you," I say. "I'll run up and check on her."

"Want me to go with you?" Lila asks.

"That's all right. I'll be right back. Y'all enjoy yourselves."

I head upstairs, stopping at the first room where Mama is staying. I knock and when there's no answer, knock again. The door opens and I step inside.

"Mama?" I call out.

The door swings shut behind me, and I turn around, startled.

"Hello, CeCe."

"What—who are you?" As soon as the words have left my mouth, I recognize her. Her hair is completely different, blonde, her makeup soft and unassuming in contrast to the bold brunette who had approached me in the restaurant the day I had lunch with Lila.

"You don't recognize me?" she asks. "I've been told I look a lot like you. Do you agree?"

"How did you get in here?" I ask, confused, and then I realize she's dressed as a member of the catering staff. "Who let you in?"

"I've been here all evening. Turns out it's not that difficult to get past those high-tech cameras y'all installed. Not if you're coming in as someone who's expected."

"If you don't leave this house right now, I'm going to call the police," I say in as even a voice as I can manage. "Clearly, you're crazy."

"Now, is that nice? Crazy? Just because I'm in love with your husband? You're in love with him. Are you crazy?"

"Get out."

"I can't do that. Not until I've accomplished what I came for."

"What are you talking about?" I say, my voice rising.

"It's unfortunate, but I really need for you to be out of the picture. I intended for this to be a seamless kind of thing. But then you turned down the wine and I had to come up with Plan B. It would have been much easier with the antifreeze."

I feel the blood leave my face. "You're kidding, right?"

"Actually, no, I'm not. The party would have been over before you started feeling bad, and you could have died in Holden's arms. Tragic, but something he could eventually come to accept I think."

I shake my head. "I'm pregnant," I say as much to myself as to her. "How could you—"

"No one wants to do these things, CeCe. But sometimes we just don't have a choice if we hope to get the things we want in life. You pick the most tasteful of distasteful options."

"Charlotte," I say, reaching for reason, "you are going to permanently mess up your life if you don't turn around and leave this room right now."

"To the contrary, I will finally be making it right. You have no idea what kind of life the rest of us lead. You in your cushioned, protected, pampered world. You won the lottery. Do you know how many people come to this city with the same dreams you had? And how many of them never even get a chance to live it out?"

"Don't try to turn this into something it's not. This is about your own desire to have something that isn't yours."

Charlotte laughs. "I'm just making a point. You've had more than your share of good fortune, right?"

"You need help," I say. "Why don't you let us find someone for you to see? It's not too late for you to make another choice. I will help you do that, Charlotte."

She reaches into the white apron tied around her waist and pulls out a long knife that I recognize as coming from our kitchen. She holds it up, saying, "I need you to do something for me, CeCe. Walk over to where I am."

"No," I say.

"Come over here and open the door. If you scream, I will be forced to stab you. And I will do my best to put the knife straight into your stomach."

I feel the blood drain from my face. My mind races for some other way to get out of the room. But there is none.

"Open the door, and we'll both walk downstairs. Do it now, or I'm coming after you with this knife. I think you can see by the length of the blade, I'm not likely to miss."

I close my eyes and draw in a deep breath. Dear God, please let someone come upstairs. Please let someone come looking for me.

I walk slowly toward her, my hands crossed protectively across my belly. If I can just get through the door, I'll have a chance to get away from her.

"That's good," she says. "Now open the door. And remember if you scream—"

"I won't," I say, turning the knob.

"That's good," she says, right behind me now, the tip of the knife against the center of my back.

I step into the hall. The stairs are fifteen feet or so ahead. I can hear the buzz of conversation and music coming from the living room below.

"Go on," Charlotte says.

I walk to the top of the staircase and stop. "I'm not going down with that knife in my back."

"You don't have a choice."

I have to get it away from her. At least knock it from her hand so I can run. "Okay," I say. "Are we going?"

"Right behind you."

And then everything happens so fast. I hear the knife clatter to the floor, just as Charlotte reaches out to push me. I start to fall forward, tripping on the step, my arms flailing for something to grab onto. She stumbles into me, and I grab onto her dress.

We're falling into nothingness. I land on my knees and start to tumble down the stairs. Charlotte falls onto me, and our weight propels us both down, down, down. My leg twists and bends behind me. I scream from the pain.

I grab for a baluster, stopping myself so abruptly that I hear my arm snap.

Charlotte continues to roll down the stairs, the thump, thump, thump of her body hitting each stone step until she lands at the bottom. People are running to the staircase now. Screams echo through the house.

"Someone call 911!"

"Oh, my God!"

I stare at Charlotte's body. Her head is bent at an alarming angle.

All I can think is that she looks like a broken doll. Once loved. Long discarded.

And her eyes are wide open.

♪

Nashville - Book Nine - You, Me and a Palm Tree

THE NASHVILLE SERIES
BOOK NINE

you, me
and a
palm tree

RITA® AWARD WINNING AUTHOR

INGLATH
COOPER

Get in Touch With Inglath Cooper

Email: inglathcooper@gmail.com
   Facebook – Inglath Cooper Books
   Instagram – inglath.cooper.books
   Pinterest – Inglath Cooper Books
   Twitter – InglathCooper
   Join Inglath Cooper's Mailing List and get a FREE ebook! Good
Guys Love Dogs!

Books by Inglath Cooper

Swerve

The Heart That Breaks

My Italian Lover

Fences – Book Three – Smith Mountain Lake Series

Dragonfly Summer – Book Two – Smith Mountain Lake Series

Blue Wide Sky – Book One – Smith Mountain Lake Series

That Month in Tuscany

And Then You Loved Me

Down a Country Road

Good Guys Love Dogs

Truths and Roses

Nashville – Part Ten – Not Without You

Nashville – Book Nine – You, Me and a Palm Tree

Nashville – Book Eight – R U Serious

Nashville – Book Seven – Commit

Nashville – Book Six – Sweet Tea and Me

Nashville – Book Five – Amazed

Nashville – Book Four – Pleasure in the Rain

Nashville – Book Three – What We Feel

Nashville – Book Two – Hammer and a Song

Nashville – Book One – Ready to Reach

On Angel's Wings

A Gift of Grace

RITA® Award Winner John Riley's Girl

A Woman With Secrets

Unfinished Business

A Woman Like Annie

The Lost Daughter of Pigeon Hollow

A Year and a Day

About Inglath Cooper

RITA® Award-winning author Inglath Cooper was born in Virginia. She is a graduate of Virginia Tech with a degree in English. She fell in love with books as soon as she learned how to read. "My mom read to us before bed, and I think that's how I started to love stories. It was like a little mini-vacation we looked forward to every night before going to sleep. I think I eventually read most of the books in my elementary school library."

That love for books translated into a natural love for writing and a desire to create stories that other readers could get lost in, just as she had gotten lost in her favorite books. Her stories focus on the dynamics of relationships, those between a man and a woman, mother and daughter, sisters, friends. They most often take place in small Virginia towns very much like the one where she grew up and are peopled with characters who reflect those values and traditions.

"There's something about small-town life that's just part of who I am. I've had the desire to live in other places, wondered what it would be like to be a true Manhattanite, but the thing I know I would miss is the familiarity of faces everywhere I go. There's a lot to be said for going in the grocery store and seeing ten people you know!"

Inglath Cooper is an avid supporter of companion animal rescue and is a volunteer and donor for the Franklin County Humane Society. She and her family have fostered many dogs and cats that have gone on to be adopted by other families. "The rewards are endless. It's an eye-opening moment to realize that what one person throws away can fill another person's life with love and joy."

Follow Inglath on Facebook
at www.facebook.com/inglathcooperbooks

Join her mailing list for news of new releases and giveaways at www.inglathcooper.com

Made in the USA
Las Vegas, NV
13 October 2022

57189129R00088